A TEXAS
THREE STEP

MIKE SALAZAR

Copyright © 2012 Mike Salazar

All rights reserved.

ISBN: 1477421807

ISBN 13: 9781477421802

Library of Congress Control Number: 2012908298
CreateSpace, North Charleston, SC

Authors Note

The idea behind writing *A Texas Three Step* came about from a conversation my wife and I had concerning a distant relative of hers named Quanah Parker. He was a Comanche warrior chief during the frontier days of the Texas plains. It is believed that he had as many as eight wives, but history can confirm he had no less than two. Later in life, he converted to Christianity. They told him that in order to live a rich and fruitful life as a Christian, he would have to choose only one wife, to which he replied, "You tell that to them. Tell me which I love the most. Tell me which one loves me the most. Tell me which one will cry the most after I send her away. Then I'll pick'em." From there my curiosity of plural marriage began.

I realize that not everyone will agree with the books core message, but I hope that it will leave you asking questions like "Is it possible?" I hope that you will take the time to conduct your own research and find the answers you are looking for. But most importantly, I hope that when you do unveil the truth, that you understand that love is not a crime.

Having said that, I would like to thank you for reading this book and embarking with me on this journey through the lives of the characters within it. So whether you bought it yourself or it was given to you, I appreciate you taking the time to read it and hope that you find it interesting enough to tell your friends about it. I do not, nor will I ever consider myself to be a great writer by any means, but I do however have a knack for telling a story in a way that most people can understand.

Lastly, I would also like to thank my wife Jennifer for being my inspiration throughout this entire process. Without her, writing this book would not have been possible. I love you babe!

Sincerely,
Mike Salazar

A Texas Three Step written by Mike Salazar

1.	How They Met	1
2.	The Proposal	9
3.	Fernando Tells Paulina	17
4.	Celina Says Goodbye	29
5.	Becoming A Texan	41
6.	They Prepare To Meet	51
7.	The Tour	67
8.	A Night To Remember	75
9.	Settling In	85
10.	Discovery	95
11.	Celina Meets The Parents	105
12.	A Truth Unfolds	119
13.	The Big Show	127
14.	Coming Out	139
15.	Here, Lies, Truth	147
16.	Face Off	159
17.	A New Life	169
18.	Undying Love	179

CHAPTER ONE

How They Met

Fernando was idly walking down the cool corridors of an art gallery in New York City, trying to decide between a colorful mosaic depicting an empty bar room and a modern still life of a rustic landscape when a quiet buzzing in his pocket interrupted his train of thought. A short text message from his friend Andy was displayed on his phone:

"Meet me outside ASAP!"

Fernando frowned as he began to type out his response, perturbed at being ordered to do something instead of being asked to: "I'm working. Can't it wait?"

Before he could finish his annoyed reply, another pulsing vibration from his phone let him know that he was being bothered once again.

"You've got to see this!" the message exclaimed.

Fernando rolled his eyes in exasperation, wondering what kind of bad sales pitch his buddy had in store for him this time. He glanced over the paintings once more, reminding himself that he was here for tasteful art and nothing else as he walked outside to meet Andy.

The lopsided grin on his friend's face was shared by his companions who were standing there apparently tipsy from the generosity of the open bar inside. Fernando told Andy he had three seconds to tell him what was so important that it couldn't wait.

Andy grinned wider and hiccupped, "I want you to meet someone—"

He turned to a pretty, dark-haired girl of about twenty-five who was standing shyly just behind him.

"Celina Santa Cruz, this is Fernando De La Mar, the art dealer from Texas I was telling you about."

She smiled despite her obvious timidity and held out her finely-shaped hand. Fernando was temporarily taken aback at her natural beauty but carefully regained his composure as he gently grasped her hand in his and slowly brought it to his lips.

"Hi, Celina, it's nice to meet you."

"Likewise," she replied, and then quickly pulled her hand away.

Fernando felt the dampness of her fingertips and smirked to himself at the thought of intimidating such a beautiful stranger.

He leaned toward Andy and whispered, "What are you doing? You know I'm here on business. I won't go back without something for my gallery." Andy refused to allow his happy buzz to be ruined and replied sluggishly, "I know, but you've been working so hard, and I just figured you might need a break!"

He boorishly slung his arm around Fernando. "Besides, you don't leave for a few more days, and this gorgeous young lady has invited us to hang out with her and her lovely friends at a pub nearby."

By this time, Andy was speaking so loudly that there was no mistaking the bright patches of red that appeared on Celina's cheeks. She pretended to search inside of her purse for something of great importance while Fernando attempted to untangle himself from Andy's headlock. Fernando's expression remained impassive, but he was struggling to decide whether a few drinks with a pretty stranger warranted being deterred from his work.

Andy continued to paw at him, "Come on!" he whined with a combination of whiskey and cigarette on his breath, "Drinks are on me."

Against his better judgment, and to satisfy his curiosity, Fernando reluctantly agreed. Knowing that he wouldn't be able to continue working and wouldn't be able to fall asleep if he returned to his hotel room, he hoped he could attempt to salvage the rest of the evening.

He felt Celina staring at him and deliberately made eye contact with her to watch her reaction. She nervously smiled again but didn't look away.

"So, I'll see you guys there, then?" she asked, never breaking eye contact with Fernando.

"Yeah, sure, I just need to freshen up a bit and get this guy some coffee, or else he'll be sleeping instead of dancing," Fernando replied jokingly.

Celina laughed and immediately felt awkward because of the unusually high pitch of her laughter.

"Okay, um...bye!" She waved cheerfully as she walked briskly to the other side of the street and disappeared around the corner.

Deciding that Andy was too drunk to drive, Fernando helped him into the passenger side of his new SUV.

"Who is this girl anyway?" he asked as he pulled away from the curb and into the late night traffic.

Andy explained she was one of the featured artists there that night, and her ambition was to make a name for herself in the art world. He also advised that she was thinking of moving to Texas, and he thought she might have a shot at it if she just had the right connections.

Fernando laughed and said, "Oh, yeah, that's my buddy, always looking out for others."

"Hey, this is the place!" Andy said, as he sat up straighter in his seat.

Fernando spotted the bright red of Celina's dress and her long black hair in front of a local salsa bar and parked in front of the building next to it. Celina was standing with two of her girlfriends at the entrance and smiled brightly as Fernando and Andy made their way past the line of people waiting to get in.

"Hey, guys!" she exclaimed, waving them up to the front.

"So you have connections, I see," Fernando said as they walked into the club together. "You must come here a lot."

Celina rolled her eyes and replied that if she had real connections, they would be drinking for free that night.

"My best friend, Jessica, is dating the door guy," and Celina pointed to a slim, tall woman with dark skin and curly hair kissing the gigantic bouncer at the door.

"Aah, so you're only cool by association, then?"

Celina laughed and playfully slapped his shoulder, "Be nice, or I won't dance with you!" she warned.

"Hey, no fighting in the club!" Celina's other girlfriend grabbed Celina by the waist and pulled her away from Fernando.

"This is my friend, April," Celina said in an attempt to introduce her. But April had already pushed her aside and had extended her hand to Fernando in an obvious attempt to get his full attention.

"I'm April Winters," she said coyly, "It's very nice to meet you," she stared at Fernando up and down as though he were a delectable appetizer. She had long blonde hair and bright blue eyes, and there was no mistaking her New Jersey accent and choice of clothes.

"Sounds like a porn star's name!" Andy laughed and ushered them toward the bar, ignoring the dark looks April and Celina gave him.

Jessica joined the girls at the bar just as April announced she needed to go to the bathroom and grabbed both Jessica's and Celina's arms to take them along.

Fernando marveled at how females always seemed to go the restroom in packs, rather than suffer the individual experience. Andy began to order drinks and left Fernando standing there thinking to himself, "What am I doing here? I should be in bed."

He took a small walk around the place, noting exits and where the bathrooms were located, how many bars there were, and the diverse variety of people that were dancing to the popular salsa music blaring from the deejay's podium. He finally found himself drawn to a two-person couch that was tucked to the left of the bar. Andy handed Fernando a martini and shook his head.

"Ok, ok. I get it. I shouldn't have pushed you so hard to come."

Fernando smiled back and said, "Forget it, man. I'm glad I came."

Andy spotted the girls as they came out of the restroom and went straight to the dance floor.

He put down his drink and said, "I can't pass this up. I'm going to go dance with them."

He wedged his way in between all of them while Fernando stayed back and watched as they danced. With his drink in hand, he tried to blend in with the locals.

Celina, feeling guilty about influencing Andy to drag his friend along, periodically looked over to where Fernando was sitting. She knew who Fernando was and all the connections he had. She also knew that she was not making a very good impression on someone that she was trying to gain artistic exposure from.

She left the dance floor, never breaking eye contact with him, and sat down next to him on the couch.

"So are you having a good time?" she shouted above the music.

"Oh, yeah," he said, "I just have a lot on my mind. I don't mean to come across as rude or anything."

She smiled and said with a look of child-like sincerity, "It must be tough being a man of your stature. How long will you be in town?" she asked.

"Just a few days, I hope. Or until I can find a few pieces to display in my gallery back in Texas."

"Andy didn't tell me it was *your* gallery," she said surprised.

"Yeah that's right. It's one of the largest in the Southwest. You should come see it sometime. I'll give you the grand tour when you become a famous artist," he teased, winking at her as he sipped his martini.

"Sure, sounds great," she replied, "I'll have to take you up on that. Of course, once I'm famous, I may not have the time," she fired back.

Not wanting Fernando to think he was in the midst of a business proposition, and feeling the rhythms of the music, she gently grabbed his martini and set it on a nearby side table.

"Come on, let's dance!"

He looked at her and smiled, thinking to himself, "Don't be a fool, go dance with her."

As they began to dance, he watched the way her hips moved to the rhythm of the beat, feeling her body against his, and smelling her long black hair as it grazed his face. The upbeat rhythms soon had them both sweating a little, and he found himself watching a single drop of sweat as it traveled down her neck, onto her chest, and in between her breasts.

She laughed breathlessly as the tempo of the music began to slow down, and she placed Fernando's hands onto her waist.

"I love this song," she said as her lips brushed his ear, "It's called 'Te Encontre.'"

"'I Found You,'" Fernando murmured back. "I've only heard the mariachi version of it."

Celina sighed and leaned her head against his shoulder, singing along to the lyrics. Fernando was stroking the length of her hair down her back, wondering how amazing her body must look if it was equally as pleasing to the eye as it was to the touch, when a loud belch resounded in his other ear.

Andy practically leaned on both of them and managed to slur, "All right? Tonight has been brill, but I'm feeling a bit knackered at the moment, can we have a squat before I get dickey?"

Celina stared at Fernando confused and asked, "Is he drunk?"

"Yes and no. That's Andy's way of saying he's had a blast, but he's tired and about to be sick and wants to sit down," Fernando said as he kept his friend from falling over.

"His American English gets a lot more *English* when he's drunk."

"Bollocks!" Andy exclaimed, "Just give us another drink, and we'll have another go after a few rounds. Throw in some grub and I'll be full of beans, luv!"

"Did he just say he wants some beans?" April laughed and handed Andy a napkin to wipe the sweat off of his brow, as Fernando sat him back onto the couch.

"Mmm, beans!" Jessica said as she fanned herself, "Celina you should cook for us, mami!"

Celina sensed her friend's ulterior motive and inclined her head blatantly toward Andy. "Well, I would, but I'm working on a bunch of important projects at home, and…"

Jessica and April giggled as Celina's face turned as red as her dress.

"That's alright," Fernando assured her, "My hotel has excellent room service. Besides, I wouldn't want Sir Drinks-A-Lot to ruin any of your masterpieces."

"Jerk!" Celina teased back, "You haven't seen the good stuff yet!"

"I want to see your good stuff," Andy said with his eyes closed and chin on his chest.

Fernando couldn't help himself and burst out laughing with the girls. In that spontaneous moment, he and Celina locked eyes and felt a connection.

She was young, beautiful, and funny, but most of all, intriguing. He was handsome, successful, direct, and still a gentleman. Celina felt as though she could trust him, even though she had just met him a few hours ago. She wanted to know more about him, and he felt the same for her.

As the night drew to an end, they began to say their goodbyes. She told him what a great time she'd had and asked him if he would be interested in going back to her place for a nightcap.

He exhaled and told her, "I really shouldn't. I should head back to my room. Besides, who's going to take care of my buddy Andy over there?"

Andy over hearing their conversation yelled back to them "I'm f-i-i-i-ine!"

"You see," she said, "Andy said he'd be alright."

Fernando politely declined but said they should do it some other night. She rummaged through her purse to look for her phone and said, "Well, give me your number so I can program it in my phone just in case."

Fernando watched in amusement as she cursed quietly to herself while searching through the contents of her enormous handbag, finally discovering a thin, silver cellular phone.

She smiled, aware of her awkwardness and asked childishly, "Ready?"

Fernando had completely forgotten that he was supposed to be providing his personal phone number to a complete stranger and felt a slight twinge of conscience as he thought of his wife.

"Would I be okay with my Paulina behaving this way?" The thought ran through his mind as he robotically iterated his phone number to Celina. She seemed unaware of his guilty expression as she typed the numbers into her phone.

Fernando quickly regained his composure, and when Celina looked up at him, he smiled genuinely and said, "Well, it's been fun, but I have to get some rest now. Feel free to call me tomorrow, and maybe we can do lunch."

"I'd like that! I'll give you call," Celina said and reached out to give him a hug and a polite kiss on the cheek.

Fernando accepted this as a social gesture and tried to avoid the more intimate thoughts that were playing through his mind. Fernando hailed an oncoming cab for Celina and helped her into the backseat.

He watched as she drove off, thinking to himself, "What am I getting myself into?" Fernando knew that there was something different about this young woman. The thought of making her his mistress was extremely appealing. However, her innocent nature made him feel like a first class jerk for entertaining that idea. She was a perfectly marriageable young woman and not some gold-digging prostitute, as far as he could tell.

"If only I'd met her sooner," he thought to himself and then began to argue with himself.

"Your wife is wonderful! Why would you trade her in?" his logical side debated.

"Why trade her in when you can have both? Mormons do it every day, don't they?" his illogical side countered mockingly. Fernando dismissed the remark, deciding that too much alcohol and fatigue was taking an irrational toll on his thinking.

CHAPTER TWO

The Proposal

The next morning was uneventful, and Fernando found himself checking his phone for missed calls more than usual. It was somewhat unnerving to him to be so expectant of another person's call. Then, just as he poured himself a freshly brewed cup of coffee, his phone rang. He rushed back into the living room where his phone sat on an end table.

"Hello," he answered, wondering what Celina would sound like on the phone.

"Hey, honey, what are you doing?" A familiar yet unidentified female voice greeted him.

"Who is this?" he asked.

Before she could answer, he regained his right frame of mind and realized, "Oh, shit, its Paulina!"

"Who *is* this?" She answered, offended, "It's your wife! Or had you forgotten you have one?"

He felt blood rush to his face but quickly recovered and replied assuredly, "I'm sorry, babe, I was expecting someone else. I thought you were Elizabeth Huntington, the owner of the gallery I went to last night. Anyway, what's up?"

"Not much, I just wanted to see how things were going and to see if you'll be back tonight or in the morning. Mary wanted me to go to the movies with her tonight."

The thought of having another opportunity to spend time with Celina immediately came to his mind.

"Well, I haven't found anything for the gallery so I'm going to head out with Andy one more time, and, hopefully, I'll get lucky," he said—and immediately felt like kicking himself.

"Oh, okay, let me know how that goes," Paulina said dismissively. She went on to describe her daily events while he continued to drink his cup of coffee, not really paying attention to what she was saying. He would mutter an occasional "uh-huh" when she would pause in her dialogue, all the while wondering if Celina made it home okay.

"Anyway," Paulina said, "Call or text me later."

"Alright, honey, I'll talk to you soon."

He put the phone down, then picked it up again, debating whether to call Celina or Andy. In the end, he decided it would be best to be dressed in more than just his underwear before calling either person. His freshly pressed shirt and slacks were hanging in the front closet. He quickly dressed, then gathered his wallet, cell phone, and day planner and went down to the street to a waiting cab. He thanked the hotel doorman and dialed Andy as he entered the cab.

"Wake up, man! We've got a busy day ahead of us."

"I will not wake up. And what do you mean 'we?'" Andy asked as he yawned loudly into the phone.

"Meet me outside. I'm taking you to breakfast."

In no time Andy was inside the cab with Fernando.

"I know a great place just a few blocks away," he said.

Fernando grinned at his friend while shaking his head, wondering if he even took the time to brush his teeth. Andy never missed an opportunity to be a first-class moocher. As they entered the diner, Andy was babbling on about what had happened the night before, then he paused when he noticed Fernando wasn't paying attention to his tales of ecstasy.

"So, what's up? You haven't said two words since I got in the cab with you. Are you alright?"

Fernando kept his cool, and knowing he had an image to live up to, he told Andy he was fine and that he just needed to eat.

What he didn't do was tell him how his mind was still on Celina.

A waitress came over to hand them their menus, poured them a cup of coffee, and told them what the daily specials were.

"We'll have two breakfast specials," Fernando said.

Andy chuckled and began to tell Fernando how he made out with one of the girls they had met the night before, what a great piece of ass she was, and how he couldn't remember how he got home.

"Man, don't you have a conscience?" Fernando asked incredulously.

Andy replied laughingly, "Yeah, I have it right here," and reached into his pocket, pulled out his middle finger, and showed it to Fernando.

"You're crazy," Fernando said smiling ear to ear.

The waitress came back with two plates of scrambled eggs, hash browns, and toast and began to refill their cups. Fernando told Andy what a waste of time it was being in New York since he hadn't bought anything to display at his gallery, and that he was thinking of leaving early.

Andy understood how important it was for Fernando to do what he had came to do but didn't know how to appease his friend.

"Well, I guess I could make a few calls to see if anyone knows of an upcoming show or anything," Andy offered.

Fernando saw this as an opportunity to bring up Celina. "What about that girl from last night? You said she was an upcoming artist. Do you think she might be willing to show us what she has?"

"Who? Celina?" Andy asked skeptically.

"Yeah. Why don't you call her?"

Andy began to scroll through his contacts on his cell phone to see if he knew someone who might have her number when Fernando said, "Here you go, buddy. I've got it right here. She gave it to me last night."

Thinking momentarily that Fernando may have had a go with her, Andy stared suspiciously at him .

"You son of a bitch! Why don't you call her yourself?"

"What?" Fernando asked, taken aback.

"You bonked her, didn't you?" Andy said accusingly.

Fernando, shaking his head, looked across at Andy. "No, you *idiot*. I'm married—remember?" Fernando said offended.

"R–i–i–ight," Andy said sarcastically, "So happily married that you would pass up a hot, young fox like Celina and then be too scared to call her the next day after a night of no sex. I gotcha," he winked.

"How's this for scared?" Fernando deliberately dialed her number, and the line rang only twice before she answered.

Fernando immediately stepped into his businessman role, ignoring the jeering looks Andy was giving him, and told Celina that he was interested in seeing some of her work. The excitement in her voice could not be hidden as she provided him her address and said she would be free all day if they wanted to drop by to take a look at her artwork.

Celina's studio was just a few blocks away, so they decided to walk to her building instead of hailing a cab. On the way there, Fernando spotted a gift shop and decided to have a look. He had intended to buy Paulina a souvenir but strangely found himself picking out something for Celina instead.

"Flowers? I don't think those will make it all the way back to Texas," Andy said with a puzzled look on his face.

"They're not for Paulina. They're for Celina."

"Celina? What the hell? You're bringing her flowers?"

"Yes, of course," Fernando said.

"Why?"

"Because that's what we southerners do," Fernando said with a wink.

They arrived at Celina's building and waited for her to buzz them in. They took an old freight elevator to the third floor, and Celina greeted them as they entered her apartment.

"Hey, guys! Come on in."

Celina immediately noticed the fresh bouquet of yellow roses Fernando was carrying and hesitantly asked, "Are those for me?"

"Yeah, well, I thought you might like them. Plus I wanted to apologize for being such a snob last night."

Fighting back the tears that glistened in her eyes, Celina blushed as she looked at him.

"That's so sweet. No one has ever bought me roses before. Let me grab a vase…" She gathered her flowers and picked out a cylindrical pottery jar from a worktable near a window.

"You have a nice place. It's so…New York," Andy commented while looking at the menagerie of paintings and sculptures that filled her living space. Fernando was impressed with her geometric use of the room, and how everything seemed to be exactly where it was meant to be.

"So you work from home? How clever," Fernando said.

"Thank you. Yeah, it's not much, but it's home. Plus the apartment manager is really nice. He pretty much lets me do what I want."

"No, I like it," Fernando said as he began to walk around. "I love the natural lighting from all the windows and the high ceilings. It's exactly how I imagined it."

"Can I offer you guys something to drink? I went to a coffee shop around the corner this morning and picked up some coffee called 'Southern Pecan,'" she said as she made her way to the kitchen.

"No thanks, I'm good," Andy said.

"How about you, Fernando?" She asked as she looked at him, hoping he picked up on the gesture of her picking out that particular blend.

"I'd love some," he said politely and followed her into the kitchen.

She poured him a cup of coffee, and trying extremely hard not to show her timidity, asked how long had he and Andy known each other.

"We met in college back home. Where did you go to college, Celina?" Fernando asked as he blew into his cup.

"I didn't go to college. I couldn't afford it. I like to think of myself as a student of life," she said lightly.

Fernando, picking up on the tension in her voice, immediately changed the subject and began to ask her about some of her creations. "So are any of these for sale?"

She replied with an anxious sound in her voice "Umm, yeah, they're all pretty much unspoken for, unfortunately. What exactly are you looking for?"

"I'm not sure, something out of the ordinary. Something with that "X" factor if you know what I mean," he said looking at her suggestively.

"I think I have just the piece you're looking for," she said picking up on his implication. "Check this out."

She made her way to another area of her studio apartment to reveal something so unique even a collector such as Fernando would appreciate it.

"Now, I hope you guys are open minded," she smiled as she began to unveil a huge clay statue of a heavenly-made naked woman riding a horse with wings and wearing nothing more than a Native American headdress. They both stared in awe, speechless, as they circled her sculpture.

"Impressive, isn't it?" She said smugly, "I call her 'Sky Rider.'"

Knowing the time and effort it must have taken her to make such a piece, Fernando searched for something to say.

"Wow. This is really good." He continued to walk around it slowly, trying not to reveal just how impressed he really was. "Where do you find your inspiration?"

"In my dreams, mostly," she said, "They are so vivid and far from reality. I can't help but grab a pen and paper and immediately write down or sketch what it was I dreamt of. From there, I either grab a paintbrush and blank canvas, some clay, or maybe even my camera and take a walk around and shoot different parts of the city."

"Well, I'm sold," Andy said. "Listen, I don't want to be rude or anything, but I have really got to go. I have to get ready for a lunch date I promised I would have with this girl I met a few weeks ago. I'll just leave you two to it." He pecked Celina on the hand.

"Call me later, Fern, and let me know what you decide."

Andy's departure left Fernando and Celina sharing an awkward silence. Fernando gazed around her studio, enjoying the amount of originality in her work. Then it came to him that maybe he could persuade her to allow him to display everything on a consignment-type basis.

He turned confidently to Celina and said, "Okay, let's get down to business. I have a proposition for you."

"So soon?" she asked jokingly.

He smiled momentarily but returned to his brisk, business manner.

"I am very interested in your work and would like to display it at my gallery. But I don't want to purchase any of it."

"What do you mean?" she asked, confused.

"Well," he explained, "You mentioned to me last night, you want to move to Texas, right?"

"Yes," she said cautiously, unsure of anything she had told him. Between the alcohol and her constant feeling of awkwardness, she could've said she was the queen of France for all she could remember.

"What if I pay to have *all* of your work shipped to Texas, and I pick up the tab for all of your moving expenses? When we have a customer for one of your pieces, I will pay you your asking price, and then I keep the difference between that and whatever price I negotiate with the customer."

He hesitated before explaining further, trying to read the expression on her face.

"Well, I'm not quite sure I understand!" She said anxiously.

"My wife and I have a really large home on about five acres of land just outside of Fort Worth. We also have a newly remodeled guesthouse in the back that is about the size of this apartment. You are more than welcome to live in it, if you like, until you find your own place."

He began to tell her of all the guesthouse's amenities when she interrupted him and said, "Your *wife*? You didn't tell me you were married," she looked at him accusingly, then immediately felt embarrassed. "Of course," she thought to herself cynically, "the first attractive, successful man I come into contact with in months would have to be married!" She recalled the last experience in which she had been remotely intimate with a man had been nothing more than a bittersweet goodbye kiss.

"Yes, her name is Paulina. We've been married for ten years," he finished lamely, feeling foolish for not mentioning it sooner. She sat on a barstool, holding her head, reviewing how she'd been behaving with a married man.

He continued to explain his intention for that particular art piece was to display it outside of the gallery. It would be the first and last artwork people would see at a one-woman show he would hold in her honor.

Biting her bottom lip with her head turned slightly to the side, she contemplated everything he had said.

"So, let me get this straight. I move down to Texas and live and work in your guesthouse rent free, and you'll pay for my moving expenses?"

"Yes. And you get to display and sell all of your work through my gallery. What better exposure could you ask for?

I'll have to think about it," she replied slowly.

"Good! You have until the end of the week to get back with me."

"I just have one other question," she said as they both made their way toward the elevator.

"Shoot!" He said.

Still confused, she put her hands on her hips and said, "What will your wife say of all this?"

He answered with confidence, "I'm not sure, exactly. You just leave that one up to me."

She smiled as he closed the gate to the freight elevator and watched him make his way down. She giggled as he continued to wave at her until he was out of eyesight. Celina felt a rush of excitement as the impact of his offer sunk in. Yet she also felt a twinge of guilt and fear. So many things had happened in such a short amount of time; it was hard for her to know what to feel first.

And the biggest shock of all was that Fernando had a wife!

Celina wondered what kind of woman she was, and what she must look like. After all of his obvious stares and the way he caressed her body as they danced, Celina was sure he was attracted to her physically. She mused that his wife must be one of those cowgirls that grew up in the country and knew very little of the big city. Celina did a quick pirouette and then ran back to her apartment to scream out her excitement into one of her pillows.

CHAPTER THREE

Fernando Tells Paulina

Fernando hailed a cab and texted his wife to let her know he was coming home and should be leaving in about an hour. He stopped back at the hotel to pick up his luggage, then was off to the airport.

Once in the air, he sipped on a glass of wine to settle his nerves. Then, at his first opportunity, he used the phone on the plane and called his wife again to let her know he was safely in the air and on his way home.

"Hey babe, it's me. I'm on my way back and wanted to know if you would like to go out to dinner tonight at Del Frisco's."

"Sure, that sounds great," she replied.

"Perfect. We have a lot to talk about," he said, "The trip turned out to be a success after all."

"Did you find what you were looking for?" she asked.

"Yeah. I did, as a matter of fact. I'll tell you all about it tonight over dinner. I'm just too tired to get into it right now."

"Ok, sweetie. I understand,." she replied. "See you tonight."

Paulina greeted him at the door and got the hug and kiss that she had longed for since he left.

He took off his hat and sat down in his favorite leather chair, saying with a soft voice, "I am so glad to be home. I hate being without you."

She replied in a sarcastic voice, "Yeah, right," as she snuggled in with him with on the chair.

"I bet you had a good time. After all, you did hang out with Andy, right? And we all know what a man-whore he is."

Fernando could only smile, and, as he had no good defense for his friend, he agreed, "Well, you got me there."

Paulina sensed he was tired and said, "We don't have to go out to dinner tonight. I know you probably just want to rest. Why don't we go out some other time?"

But Fernando stubbornly objected, "No, honey, let's go out. Anyway, I have a lot to talk to you about. I could use a steak."

"Okay," she replied trying to hide her enthusiasm. She pecked him on the cheek telling him softly, "I'll start getting ready. Why don't you take a quick nap or something while I get in the shower? Don't forget to call and make reservations. You know what happened last time."

"Okay, babe, I will," he said to her as he looked around trying to remember where he put his cell phone. He grabbed his coat, fumbled through the pockets, and found his cell phone still on vibrate with two missed call from Andy, and a short text from Celina.

He immediately read her text message that said, "Had a great time. Still thinking about the offer. Hope you made it home okay. Call me later whenever you get a chance."—she ended the text with a smiley face.

He grinned ear to ear as he read the message knowing the offer he made to her was too attractive for her to turn down. He decided to wait to return Andy's call assuming if it were that important, he would have left a message.

Fernando called to make reservations but was too restless to take a nap. Instead, he decided to surprise Paulina by jumping in the shower with her. Fernando quietly opened the bathroom door and lit every candle before dimming the lights.

"What are you up to now?" she called out to him. He removed his clothes and pulled the shower curtain aside, admiring his wife's familiar curves.

"May I join you, ma'am, or is your husband going to be home soon?" he said, trying to impersonate one of their younger lawn attendants.

She laughed and replied, "Why, yes, that would be sweet. I need a strong man's help while my husband is away," she giggled as he stepped into the shower's warm jets. He shivered a little and pulled her wet body close to him.

"Geez, could you have it any colder in here?" he asked as he turned up the hot water.

"Well, I thought I could warm you up myself," she said and began to kiss him along his jaw line.

He ran his hands over her hips and kissed her long and deep. The heat from the water began to fill the room with steam as their touching became more passionate. As his hands caressed her body, Paulina responded eagerly, pressing herself against him harder.

Although she had grown accustomed to his long absences, it did not diminish her desire for him. Fernando was equally aroused and intended to release all of the repressed sexual yearnings his time away had caused. He kissed her slowly down her neck and continued to follow the water's trail until she was begging him to make love to her. He grasped her firmly by the waist as she wrapped her legs around him. He entered her slowly at first, enjoying the heat and moisture both inside and outside. Her moans of pleasure encouraged him to move faster until they both exploded. Trembling, she reached out to turn the water off.

"What's gotten into you?" she gasped, trying to catch her breath.

"Did you not like it?" he asked, equally out of breath. "I'm not one to complain, but seeing as how we haven't had sex like that in months, I have to wonder where this is coming from," she smiled. "Have I lost weight or something?"

Fernando laughed and handed her a bathrobe while he fastened a towel around his waist, "Can I not be happy to see my beautiful wife after a long, boring trip?"

Paulina smirked and replied, "I'll take that compliment," then headed to her apartment-sized closet to get dressed. Having that kind of sexual encounter was not a part of their normal lifestyle. It was unusual for them to behave that way, but she was not about to ruin it by over analyzing it.

Paulina was an only child and her parents never discussed sex with her freely. The type of role playing that she and her husband did was a new aspect for her erotically.

"Are we taking the Mercedes or the Rover tonight?" Fernando asked as he surveyed the different keys on his desk. "The Mercedes!" Paulina called out as she walked downstairs, taking care not to step on the beaded hemline of her new evening dress.

Fernando smiled, knowing the Mercedes was her favorite, as it had been her Christmas present from the previous year. She had also hinted that there was certain silver Audi at the new dealership a few blocks from their home that had caught her eye, but Fernando was not going to indulge her in something she would have no use for.

He rather thought of hiring a personal chauffeur, which would also save him the trouble of tagging along on some of her more boring endeavors, but he knew if she ever found out that he thought anything she did was "boring," he would never hear the end of it.

He could almost hear her mother's nagging voice, "I told you that you shouldn't have married such a serious man!"

He quickly grabbed the keys and headed outside, as if trying to escape the very thought of his mother-in-law. Paulina was idly searching in her silver clutch for something and talking quietly to herself. The image reminded Fernando of his first meeting with Celina, and he wondered what a woman could possibly place inside her handbag that always required such an arduous search. She smiled as he opened her door and helped her carefully tuck her dress in before shutting it.

Before long, they were driving toward downtown Fort Worth with the radio playing softly in the background. Fernando absentmindedly changed the stations and didn't attempt to make small talk. Paulina noticed his fidgety behavior but didn't speak of it. When they arrived, he valet-parked the car, looked up, and groaned in exasperation.

"Do we really have to speak to them?" he asked, as the Wellesley's, neighbors that lived two miles west of them, were smiling and walking toward them.

"Ferny, be nice!" Paulina whispered, "They are on the historic preservation society's council, so if you want their support when you bring back junk from East Texas, you better smile and compliment her shoes or something."

Mr. Wellesley grasped Fernando's hand and clapped him heartily on the back, "Seen-yore Day La Mar! How's pickin's?" he asked, which was his usual greeting for Fernando.

"Pretty slim there, friend," Fernando replied and reached for Paulina, "But I still think I have the best one made, next to yours, of course" he let his lips briefly touch Mrs. Wellesley's hand as she smiled and turned to Paulina.

"Wherever did you get that dress? It's just beautiful!" Mrs. Wellesley exclaimed.

"I've had this old thing in my closet for a month," Paulina replied nonchalantly. "I just love your earrings!"

Mrs. Wellesley laughed and said equally nonchalantly, "We've had these old things in our family for years."

Paulina forced out a polite laugh and looked over at Fernando to make sure he was on his best behavior. Mr. Wellesley asked Fernando how his business was doing while Mrs. Wellesley told Paulina not to leave without trying the six-ounce governor's filet.

Fernando let out a sigh of relief as they said their goodbyes and entered the restaurant.

The hostess looked like a high school student but greeted them professionally and asked their name. "De La Mar, party of two," Fernando advised.

"De La Mar? Like the art gallery?" she asked astonished. Paulina smiled at Fernando, admiring his poise and reserve as he politely acknowledged the young hostess's query.

"Yes, just like the art gallery. Are you a fellow art lover?" he asked.

The girl turned a considerable shade of bright pink and replied, "Oh yes, very much! I'm a street artist, but no one considers street art, ART, ya know? I'm going to be taking formal art classes at TCU next year, but I don't want to give up on my passion, and..." the girl's excited speech was cut short when she saw the annoyed look on Paulina's face.

"I'm sorry, I don't mean to keep you from your dinner. Right this way, please!"

Fernando thanked her and handed her a business card before allowing her to walk away. "You should stop by the gallery in a few weeks. I'll have some exciting new pieces by then, and, maybe one day, I'll be showing off some of yours." He winked as the girl blushed even deeper and accepted his card.

Paulina rolled her eyes but was only slightly perturbed. Having young women fall all over themselves in Fernando's presence was not an uncommon thing. After all, he was a very handsome man and quite charming when he wanted to be. Fernando attempted to smile innocently.

"There is nothing wrong with wanting to support our local artists," he said as he began to look over the wine menu.

Fernando ordered a bottle of cabernet sauvignon. As the waitress began to pour their wine, Fernando felt his palms start to sweat. He contemplated in his mind how he was going to bring up the proposal he had made to Celina. Paulina knew something was weighing on his mind and stretched out her hand to his.

"What's wrong, babe? Are you okay?"

"I'm fine," he replied, and began to nervously sip from his glass without setting it down. Paulina looked at him quizzically and then began to describe her day with her friend Mary. As she began to go into detail about the characters of the movie they saw, Fernando's hidden anxiety caused him to interrupt her monologue.

"So I have some interesting and exciting news," he said quickly in between sips of his wine. Just then the waitress came over to take the rest of their order, and Fernando stuttered as he told the waitress, "We'll both have the veal chops with asparagus, please."

Paulina was beginning to grow annoyed with Fernando's strange behavior, but calmly asked, "Really? Well, what is it?"

"My trip to New York," he began and swallowed the lump that had grown in his throat.

"Yes?" she asked with a calculating look on her face.

"I think I've discovered a new talent. Andy introduced me to a friend of his whose work was very impressive, and I've offered to do an exhibition at the gallery."

"Oh, really? That's great!" She said enthusiastically, relieved that he was not delivering what she thought was going to be bad news. "What's his name? Do I know him?"

"No, I don't think so," he said carefully. "Her name is Celina Santa Cruz. She's from Brazil."

"A female friend of Andy's?" she replied coolly, staring skeptically at her husband, aware of what her facial expressions were conveying.

"It's not what you think," Fernando began to explain. "I thought the same thing at first, but she's actually very talented. In fact, that's what I wanted to talk to you about."

"You see, Celina has been working in and around New York ever since her mom died some time ago, and now she's actually thinking of moving here to Texas. She was kind enough to show Andy and me her private collection at her studio, and you know me, I'm not easily impressed. But I have to admit, she had quite an array of artwork. There was this one piece she had that was so impressive that I could imagine it right in front of the gallery."

"What is it?" Paulina said having now got her full attention.

"Well, it's actually pretty cool," he replied, trying to read Paulina's body language, "It's a really big sculpture of a naked woman wearing an Indian headdress riding a wild stallion with wings."

"Oh wow, that does sound interesting," Paulina said sarcastically, "How much is it going to cost us?"

Fernando, knowing that Paulina controlled all aspects of the galleries expenses cleared his throat and replied, "Well, that's the best part. It's free."

Free?" she asked skeptically. "Nothing is ever free, Fernando. What's the catch?"

Fernando knew better than to keep beating around the bush. "You know how I told you she is planning on moving to Texas? Well, I thought it might be a good opportunity for all of us if she were to move in with us for a while," he said as he called the waitress over to pour another glass of wine.

"Wait a minute, you've invited a complete stranger to stay in our *home*? And without consulting me?" she asked in disbelief.

"Celina has an entire apartment and studio that she will have to move down here, and, of course, the cost of moving a load that big, including sculptures and paintings, would be too great. Plus we have the guesthouse outside that we don't even use. It's a win-win situation. She gets a fresh start down here, and we get to add a new artist and have a new exhibit.

You see, we'll display all of her work on consignment and pay her when it sells. Think of it like an investment in our future."

Unconvinced, Paulina glared at him "Well, *if* I were to agree to this, when were you thinking of making all this happen?"

"Right away," Fernando said firmly, unhappy that Paulina was not as enthusiastic as he had thought she would be.

Fernando and Paulina ate their dinner in silence. Paulina began to think of what her husband was asking her to consider. Paulina was in charge of all the aspects of the company and allowed Fernando to have the artistic freedom to choose what pieces would be displayed. She knew that something like this could be exactly what they needed to get some much-needed exposure—a rival gallery was featuring new, younger talent.

From a business standpoint, Fernando may have made a choice that made sense. However, from a personal standpoint, no man in his right mind would ever make the decision to invite a woman into his wife's home without her knowledge or permission. Paulina would have liked to mention that if she had done such a thing, Fernando would have been more than bothered by the idea.

Neither one of them had ever been unfaithful in their entire relationship, even before they were married. Fernando had always expressed his love and devotion to Paulina so for her to think that he would compromise their relationship would be out of character for her, in his opinion.

Besides, Celina would not be living inside the house, and with their busy schedules, it would be unlikely they would see her that often.

Fernando attempted to get Paulina thinking of something else; he was remarking on how good his veal chops were when suddenly Paulina interrupted him.

"You know, this may not be a bad idea," she said, careful of her tone. She intended to call his bluff. If the artist turned out to be as good as he said, then she wouldn't have a problem finding her own place in a matter of weeks, while in the meantime earning a nice profit for their gallery.

If she was only the kind of artist that a skirt-chasing pig like Andy would befriend, then she could easily find a reason to send her back to wherever her husband had found her—, and maybe him along with her.

"I'm glad you think so," Fernando said, amazed at his skills of persuasion.

"I'll have to speak with her about all of this and also do a formal background check." Paulina said as she began to scroll through her Blackberry, "What about Thursday? I'm free on Thursday."

"Okay," he said. "I'll give her a call tomorrow and see if she is still interested in our offer."

As they finished their meal, Fernando felt a wave of relief that the hard part was over. He had been honest and appreciated Paulina for being open-minded to the offer he made to Celina.

Paulina was still contemplating what they had talked about and refused to make eye contact. He pulled his chair in closer and began to tell her that he loved her very much. Paulina stared at him quietly, then forced herself to smile at him.

"I know we haven't spent much time together recently," he said remorsefully. "But who knows what the future has in store for us? Things will get better. You'll see." Fernando was always out of town trying to find new art to sell at their gallery. Paulina longed for him to be with her more, but she had to stay back and tend to the gallery itself. His idea, while unconventional, was beginning to appeal to her but mostly because it would allow him to be at home more often.

After leaving the restaurant, Fernando took the long way home without realizing it. They didn't say much to each other, but each was thinking the same thing—that something was missing in their lives. Paulina was unsure if this was some kind of mid-life crisis that Fernando may be going though. Instead of getting a brand new sports car like most middle aged men would, he wanted to bring another woman into their home. She was surprised to realize that she did not feel an ounce of jealousy. The feeling that overwhelmed her was the disappointment of thinking she was not a sufficient wife or partner.

Fernando glanced over at his wife, wishing he could read her mind. He was sure the secrets of her heart were things he would never fully understand. The cold, unhappy look on her face made him feel like a stranger sitting next to her. She reached out to adjust the car temperature on her side of the vehicle and the sight of her wedding ring made him think of Celina. He recalled how she had worn no jewelry, not even earrings as they danced that night. He hastily reached out to grasp Paulina's hand in his, in an attempt to remove Celina from his mind.

As they pulled into the driveway of their home, Fernando carefully parked the car inside their garage, then made his way to open Paulina's door for her. He extended his hand, pulled her closely to him and attempted to kiss her, trying to rekindle their earlier passion. Paulina gently pushed him away and said, "Not now. Not like this."

She walked into the house and headed straight to their bedroom alone, leaving him speechless in the driveway. Fernando was completely frustrated and kicked his car tire.

"Why doesn't she love me? I give her everything she wants and still I'm not good enough for her. She's just a spoiled bitch who doesn't appreciate me," he thought to himself as he went into the house and threw his keys on the kitchen counter.

He walked to his study and sat down in front of his computer. Attempting to distract himself, he began to go through his e-mails. He grabbed a bottle of scotch that was on a mini bar next to his desk and poured himself a drink. He swallowed it in one gulp, and then poured another. His inbox was flooded with events and reminders from Paulina. He chuckled to himself as he thought of the lectures she would give him if he didn't respond or confirm her messages within ten minutes of receiving them.

He checked off the receipt requests and deleted them, knowing it would infuriate her, and she would retaliate by resending them. He poured himself another drink then slammed his laptop shut, as if trying to shut out the sound of her nagging. He leaned back in his chair, and his eyes rested on a large, framed photo of them on their wedding day: it was the centerpiece of his floor to ceiling bookshelves.

Paulina was so young and vibrant then. They both were. His thoughts travelled back to that day, and how nervous he had been. He knew her parents weren't thrilled about their union and viewed him as unsuitable because he was not in the same class as their privileged family. He knew his own mother was also worried that he would forget his roots as he married into such a wealthy family, and even more that Fernando would turn his back on the family that loved him.

He knew he didn't have anything to offer this beautiful woman that she didn't already have. And yet, he remembered seeing her walk down the aisle, with tears streaming down her face, smiling at him and never breaking her gaze. Fernando sighed slowly as his heart felt a familiar stab. He knew she loved him in that moment. When her father placed her hand in his, Fernando felt an overwhelming sense of protection like never before. He would die for this woman.

Just weeks before their wedding, they had made a plan to elope without telling anyone due to Paulina's parents making all of the wedding preparations without consulting their daughter or him. They felt it was their right to give the wedding they desired, since they were paying for everything.

Fernando smiled as he remembered receiving a call from a distraught Paulina at two o'clock in the morning demanding that he pick her up right that second, and then fly the two of them to Vegas to get married in a drive-up chapel with Elvis as their witness.

Fernando managed to calm her down and reminded her that the details of their wedding didn't matter to him. What mattered was that they would be together. He had picked her up, and they drove to a secluded spot. Then, they made love under the stars.

Paulina had said it was one of the most romantic moments of her life. Fernando frowned as it dawned on him that he could not remember her saying that to him since then. Maybe he wasn't being as great of a husband as he thought he was, and maybe she wasn't such a spoiled bitch after all. He raised his glass of scotch, toasted their picture, and then swallowed it down. He slowly walked to their bedroom, thinking of the right words for a good apology.

As he opened the door, he saw that Paulina was already asleep. He sighed and undressed, then slowly lay down next to her. He curled himself around her, spooning her into his body. He whispered, "I'm sorry," into her hair and felt her hand slide into his. He kissed the back of her head and then drifted to sleep.

The next day, Paulina woke up a little later than usual. Anita, their maid of ten years, was knocking quietly, "Senora, breakfast is ready."

Paulina looked over at her clock and was amazed to see it was almost nine o'clock. "We're getting up!" she called out to Anita. Fernando rolled over to hug Paulina and threw his leg over her torso. Paulina groaned and pushed his leg off, telling him to stay on his side of the bed.

Fernando couldn't help but smile as he knew everything they had fought about the night before was behind them now. She went into the bathroom and turned on the radio to catch her favorite morning talk show and turned on the shower.

Paulina let the warm water course down her body and willed the tension of the night before to be washed away from her, as if it were soap suds. She knew if she dwelled on the negativity of their relationship, she would begin a downward spiral into a deep depression.

She had already accepted the fact that she devoted her younger years to their partnership, both business and romantic. Fernando had never pressured her about having or not having children. They had lost some pregnancies and were both older now; the prospect of having a child was growing slimmer and slimmer. Yet, she could not help but feel a twinge of resentment toward Fernando.

He got to escape the mundane routines of home life because he was constantly travelling, meeting new people and visiting different places. Paulina, on the other hand, had to keep up appearances and attend many family functions by herself, to the disapproval of both of their families.

Paulina's friends and relatives already had children that were finishing grammar school so she felt left out at social gatherings when the topic of conversations turned to their children's accomplishments or failures.

The business of the art gallery kept her extremely occupied at times—so much so that it would interfere with the time the couple could enjoy together when Fernando wasn't travelling.

Paulina's parents were also Fernando's primary investors when the business began, so she felt obligated to continue to fortify her family's good name in their aristocratic social circles.

Paulina knew her thoughts were taking a dark turn, so she began to sing along to a pop song on the radio. As her mood improved, her singing worsened. Fernando could hear her caterwauling all the way into their bedroom and cringed in embarrassment. He wondered how could such a lovely woman have such a terrible singing voice?

CHAPTER FOUR

Celina Says Goodbye

Meanwhile back in New York, Celina awoke to warm beams of sunlight on her face and the familiar smells of clay, paint, and scented dryer sheets. She inhaled deeply, without opening her eyes, wanting to savor every memory that she could. Since Fernando made the invitation to her, she was sure she would never wake up the same way again. It would be in a different city, a different climate, and a different world.

Although she was excited to take a chance on an almost unbelievable experience, she felt a bit of bittersweet sadness. In many ways, New York had been like a first love, and she wasn't sure how she was going to let it go. Celina sighed and opened her eyes.

The cracks in the old ceiling and chipped paint were all connected in a way that reminded her of a topographical map she had seen at her grammar school in Rio de Janeiro. Geography was an important lesson due to the terrain of the country. Children had to be able to find their way if they got lost in the countryside while working. Back then, when she would wake up and open her eyes, there was a poster of New York City taped to the ceiling of her bedroom. Life's little ironies were a constant source of inspiration to her.

She rolled to her side and hugged her pillow to her chest. Her eyes rested upon the vase of yellow roses that Fernando had given her. She studied each petal and thorn, wondering if he would ever know the impact his unexpected gift had had upon her. She almost cried when he presented them to her that afternoon.

Her mother had worked in a rose factory in Brazil for years before Celina was born, shaving thorns from the stems for floral distribution companies. Her mother's hands were toughened with scars and felt like old paper when she would caress Celina's hair at night as she sang to her, but she always had that sweet, flowery smell. Celina ran her hand down the length of her pillow, feeling the stitching of the embroidered roses and butterflies.

The pillowcases were a gift from her grandmother who also worked in the factories and smelled the same as her mother. She had spent less and less time thinking of her family as her creative flow increased, because it would dampen her spirit.

Now, however, the reality of relocating again began to settle in. Her eyes welled up with tears, and she buried her face in her pillow, breathing in as hard as she could.

"Mommy," she whispered, "Watch over me please." She could see her grandmother's smiling face in her mind, and a soothing calm stopped her tears.

"I can do this," she said aloud to her apartment. The windows rattled as if in agreement.

Celina threw off her blankets and was setting out purposefully to her bathroom to begin the first day of her new life when her cell phone began ringing. The reggae ringtone let her know it was Jessica.

"Hey, mami, what's up?" she greeted her warmly.

"Nothing much, just making sure you're coming for dinner tonight. Pollo frito and arepas!"

Monday night was always reserved for Jessica's island cuisine. Celina felt troubled at the thought of breaking a tradition with her friend and said hesitantly, "Actually, I have something important and exciting to tell you."

"Uh-oh!" Jessica exclaimed surprised, "Should I sit down?"

Celina laughed, "Well, maybe you shouldn't be operating large machinery, but I think standing up is okay for now. You remember Fernando, right?"

"Yeah, what about him?" Jessica suspiciously asked.

"He wants to display my entire collection at his gallery in Texas! It will be my own exhibition, and he says he will pay for *everything*. All of my moving expenses, my artwork, and he'll even let me stay in his guesthouse for free while I work on new projects."

"That's great!" Jessica exclaimed enthusiastically. "How long will you be gone?"

Celina hesitated again before answering reluctantly, "I'm not sure, but I know I'll be leaving soon. He said I have until the end of this week to decide."

Jessica's tone became suspicious again, "What's the catch?"

"There is no catch, at least none that have surfaced," Celina replied. "Anyway, I'm glad you called because I have a great idea. I've been living here for years and have never really gotten to see or experience any other parts of the city. Do you want to be my tour guide? I'll take you to dinner so you won't have to cook!" Celina wheedled.

"Oh, alright," Jessica said grudgingly, "But you're taking me somewhere *nice*."

"We'll go wherever you want, but I'm going to the spa first so I can be extra pretty for you, mami!" Celina joked. "I'll see you around one o'clock."

When Jessica hung up the phone she wondered if the real reason Celina was so anxious about moving to Texas was so that she could be closer to that loser ex-boyfriend of hers, Jaime Mata. He had been incarcerated a year earlier on a drug trafficking charge.

As long as Jessica had known Celina, he had been a negative influence in her life. Yet, Celina always defended him to Jessica, making excuses for his bad behavior by citing everything from his poor upbringing to the economy.

Celina and Jaime started dating after he asked her out several times while on the subway on her way to work. At first, she saw him as an egotistical, arrogant younger guy who just wouldn't give up.

Against her better judgment, she finally gave in to his flirtations, and agreed to go to dinner with him. Dinner consisted of a hot dog and a cab ride to Times Square, which Celina had paid for. However, once in the middle of the busy streets, she saw him in a different light.

Every manner of working class citizen knew who he was, from waiters to bell hops to night club dancers. He appeared to come alive from all of the attention and his charming demeanor won over Celina's trepidation of being with him.

At the end of their date, he borrowed a friend's car to drive her home. As they said their farewells at her apartment door, he smiled and reached into his pocket, stating he had something for her. When she looked down to see what it was, he gripped her face firmly in his hands and kissed her so deeply, he left her breathless. When he pulled away, he whispered, "You're mine now," and Celina knew she was in love.

He never had steady work, yet he never seemed to have a problem spending money. Celina knew he must have been doing something illegal to make ends meet. When she would ask him what he did for a living, he would always dance around the question and would make it a point not to tell her anything specific.

They stayed together for a little more than a year. During the course of their relationship he cheated on her twice (that she knew of) and would mentally and verbally abuse her each time he drank. Despite his jealous tendencies and the emotional stress he would cause her, Celina stayed with him.

She refused to give up on her belief that with the right guidance and all of her love, he could be a great husband and maybe even a great father. Celina's longing to have a family was also a weakness that Jaime used to his advantage when he wanted her forgiveness.

After a particularly nasty fight, he said he was going to Texas for about a week to visit some family who lived in Houston. Little did she know that he was in fact a middleman between border town drug traffickers in south Texas and the East Coast.

She knew something had gone wrong, because she did not hear from him for about two months. Each day, she found herself searching the mail or staring listlessly at her phone, waiting to hear from him. She lost so much weight, she became anemic. Finally, she received a letter he sent from the Harris County jail. Field agents who had been watching him and his friends for months had picked up Jaime in a meth lab raid.

He told her that he was looking at no less than three years in prison for his part in the whole scheme—but steadfastly maintained his innocence.

He said he had been at the wrong place at the wrong time and tried to blame her by saying that everything he did, he did for her. Needless to say, Jessica wanted nothing to do with him and hated that Celina had been so blind and naïve about Jaime.

Jessica began to fear that her friend was getting ready to make a huge mistake and move to Texas so that she could more easily visit him in prison. She only wanted what was best for Celina. She just wished Celina could meet a man who would love and appreciate her for who she was. But she was afraid that Jaime penetrated into Celina's psyche too deep. She feared that Celina thought that no one could ever be as good as he was. She decided she would confront Celina about this fear when they met up.

Meanwhile, Celina decided to go to Spa Ja, one of New York's premiere Brazilian spas. This was somewhat of an inside joke to Celina, as she could not recall any such beauty services being sought after in her home country. Any rational woman would not want to be dipped in mud or hot wax in order to feel beautiful or rejuvenated. Rather, she would carefully watch her diet and enjoy the benefits of walking to the market instead of riding in a car or swimming in the ocean just outside of Rocihna, her family's neighborhood.

She recalled the many tourists who visited the town, which their Brazilian tour guides from the city referred to as an "urbanized slum." Those same tour guides would often purposely lead the tourists into more rural areas, rob them, and abandon them to find their way back alone. It was a hypocrisy that always amused her.

She rationalized that she was only there for a Brazilian manicure, pedicure and facial, none of which required artificial nails or chemical ingredients. She smiled at the Asian woman trimming her cuticles and reflected on the absurdity of it all. An Asian American is giving me, a natural born Brazilian American, a Brazilian manicure in a Caucasian owned spa in New York City.

"Every ting okay, honey?" the lady asked with a look of polite curiosity.

"Oh yes, perfectly," she replied, stifling a giggle. Before the technician could engage her in a more awkward conversation, Celina's phone began to ring. To her surprise, it was Fernando.

The nervous sound in her voice was portrayed to Fernando when she said "Um, Hello?"

Fernando squinted his brow and said *"Hi.* Is this Celina?"

"Yeah, this is she." She said, still frightened.

"It's me, Fernando. I hope I'm not interrupting or anything. Do you have a minute?"

"Umm, yeah," she said trying to gather her composure.

"Well, I was hoping you have had a chance to think over my offer."

"Yes, I have," she said." I just have a few questions, if you don't mind."

"Not at all, shoot!" he said confidently.

"Well first, when were you thinking of doing all of this? Because if I decide to do this, it is going to take a lot of planning on my part."

"Well, I talked to my wife Paulina about it, and truthfully, we were kind of hoping we could arrange this within the next few days."

"Okay. Well, what would I have to do?" She said trying even harder not to reveal her excitement.

"I tell you what—I will e-mail you your flight schedule today and arrange to have the movers pick up all of your things later on this week. Just bring what you need to last you a few days, and before you know it, the rest of your things will be here. I'll even make it a round trip ticket just in case you get here and decide to change your mind or something. What do you say?" he asked.

Celina, having no more excuses to give him about going, finally said, "Okay! You got yourself a deal!"

"Then it's settled," he replied. "We will see you in a couple of days."

They both hung up the phone and exhaled a sigh of relief.

Fernando immediately called his wife Paulina to tell her the news and to give her the go ahead to make all the travel arrangements.

"Hey, babe. Everything is a go with Celina."

"With what?" She asked.

"I called Celina, and she said she is looking forward to becoming a Texan. Go ahead and book a flight for her, then go online and find out how much it's going to cost us to move her stuff down here."

"Okay," she said, "But you don't have to be so demanding about it."

"I'm sorry, honey, it's just that I'm on my way to the studio now, getting ready to open, and I just received a text from Christie saying she is going to be late."

"Alright, babe. I'll do it here in a little while once I get done paying a few bills online. You know, we really have to start cutting back on a few things around here. It would make my life so much easier if I didn't have to keep up with all of your exploits," she said jokingly.

"I know babe, I know," he said rolling his eyes. "Just one more thing," he said. "Make it a round trip ticket."

"Of course," she said, keeping her motives for being so agreeable to herself.

Fernando explained his request, "Just in case she gets down here, and any of us decide that maybe it wasn't such a good idea after all. Besides, I'm more concerned about what you will think of her anyway. This way we get to 'taste the goods' so to speak, and she doesn't feel like she's totally committed just yet."

"Ha, ha," Paulina said sarcastically, "There will be no 'tasting' of anything! Get that straight, Fern! Give me her e-mail address and phone number just in case I have to reach her."

"Oh, shit! I forgot to get it. Do you have a pen?" he asked her.

"Yeah, go ahead," she said, annoyed. He gave her Celina's phone number and asked her if she could call her for him.

"I guess," she replied.

"I love you."

"Love you, too. Talk to you later."

As Celina sat there with her face full of mud, hands drying and toes being fashioned, she couldn't help to think of how much her life was about to change. She pictured herself living the dream, selling out in every art show across America, when suddenly her phone rang again. She looked at her phone and saw it was a call from Texas.

She quickly answered and said, "Hi, Fernando?"

"No, this is Paulina De La Mar. Fernando's wife."

She quickly pulled her feet from the foot spa, and apologized profusely while explaining she thought Paulina was Fernando.

A vision immediately ran through Paulina's mind, and she felt right in being reluctant to have this ditsy woman move into their estate. But Paulina decided to give Celina the benefit of the doubt.

Trying to keep her cool, she explained to Celina how Fernando told her that she accepted the offer but needed to get some information from her so she could send her a ticket.

Celina stumbled giving the information, reciting it to her three times before getting it right. Paulina laughed, sensing Celina's nervousness. To ease the tension, Paulina began to make small talk with her.

"So, Fernando said you are a friend of Andy's. How do you know him?"

"We met last summer at a pub in London while I was over there trying to sell some of my work," she said feeling a bit more at ease.

"Yeah, I really didn't do so well over there. After all, most of my works at that time were photos of the Southwest. They just didn't find those as interesting as I had hoped. Andy must have seen that look I get when I'm feeling sorry for myself and thought I looked like an easy target," she said as she laughed.

Paulina knew exactly what she was talking about and replied, "That's Andy, alright!"

"Yeah, he came over as only Andy could do, with that gleam in his eye thinking he was going to get lucky or something. He used the cheesiest pick up line I ever heard in my life." She paused.

"And what was that?" Paulina wondered how many pick up lines this female had heard over the course of her life.

"He said, 'Do you mind if I hang out here for a while until it's safe back where I farted?'"

"Oh my God, no, he didn't!" Paulina said, laughing in disbelief.

"Yes, he did." Celina said.

"And that worked?" Paulina asked.

"Well, yeah I guess it did," Celina said trying to recall why she became friends with Andy. "He's actually a really nice guy. Plus I love his British accent."

"I know it's probably none of my business," Paulina said bluntly, "But did you guys ever hook up?"

"Oh, heck no! I could pick out his type in a lineup real fast. He probably thought I was some lonely low life—excuse my French—*bitch* he could just have his way with. But I made it very clear that he was not my type, and there was no way in hell he was going to get in my pants."

"Good for you," Paulina praised her.

"Anyway, he bought me a drink or two, and we just sat at the bar getting to know each other. That's when I told him I lived in New York and invited him to the art show where he introduced me to Fernando. Andy told me that he lived in New York, too, but he was in London visiting friends and family for a couple of weeks. We've been friends ever since," Celina said.

Paulina was now feeling a bit more at ease about the whole arrangement after having spoken to Celina. She gathered all the information she needed and ended the call by saying, "Well, it's been really nice talking to you, and I am looking forward to meeting you in person real soon."

"Me, too," Celina said relieved. "You seem like a real nice person, and I can't wait to get down there."

When Paulina hung up the phone, she couldn't help thinking to herself how good it might be to have someone around to talk to when Fernando was away. After all, Paulina didn't have very many friends, and it would be nice to have someone to have a little "girl talk" with for a change. Paulina longed for a sister all her life. She thought briefly that Celina could fill that missing void she yearned for.

Celina immediately began to exhale a sigh of relief, sitting back in her chair and realizing her dreams were finally taking shape.

After leaving the salon, Celina, still excited from talking to Paulina, called her friend Jessica to begin taking in the city as they had planned. The phone rang only once before Jessica answered.

"Are you ready, bitch?"

"Hell, yeah, let's do it," Jessica said. "I've been looking forward to hanging out with you all morning long. I still can't believe your leaving me."

"So what do you want to do first?" Celina asked.

"I don't know...how about you meet me at Gray's Papaya on Broadway?"

"Okay. I could use some good wiener right about now," Celina joked.

Celina was trying to hold back mixed emotions about leaving everything behind including this friend she would miss dearly. On the taxi ride there, Celina began to recall how she met Jessica and random things they had done together over the years. She also began to feel sad about leaving New York and all the little things about living in such a big city. The sounds of the busy streets, the way people can be so rude and unsociable yet generous and kind in a crisis—and, of course, the skyline and lights of the city at night.

There was nothing that she would miss more, however, than her friend Jessica. She remembered when they first met how they really didn't like each other so much. At the time, Celina was twenty and Jessica was twenty-three. Jessica had been working in that restaurant for months before Celina began to work there.

Celina was shy and reserved. She remembered one time she was carrying a tray of appetizers to a group of people; she accidently dropped it on the floor. Some of the other wait staff saw it when it happened and began to laugh and make fun of her for being so clumsy. Jessica being the good-hearted person she was saw how embarrassed Celina looked and didn't feel right not helping her out.

While Celina was apologizing to the customers and trying to clean up the mess, Jessica went over to give her a hand. Celina told her that she had everything under control, but Jessica saw through her and assisted her anyway. Ever since then, they were like peanut butter and jelly. Both were very attractive and broke hearts wherever they went.

People would often accuse them of being intimate with each other, but despite their physical attraction to one another neither one of them ever acted on it.

Celina arrived at Gray's Papaya first so she decided to wait outside for Jessica to show. As she stood there on the sidewalk, it also began to sink in that she wasn't so much leaving something behind, but that she was going to make a new start and meet new friends as well as bettering her career.

Before long, Jessica showed up smiling ear to ear at her best friend, jumped out of the cab, and ran to Celina to give her a hug.

"I'm going to miss you!" Jessica said as she began to tear up.

"I'm going to miss you, too," Celina replied. "But, hey, I'm only going to be a phone call or e-mail away so you better not forget me."

"I won't," she said still fighting her emotions. "And hey, if everything works out, I'm going to try and visit you this summer."

"Okay. I'm going to hold you to that."

During lunch they decided to go to the Museum of Modern Art (or MoMA) to take one last glimpse of one of the greatest museums in America that was just a few blocks away. They took the short ride to the museum, and on the way there they held each other's hands and talked each other's ears off about any and everything they could think to say—and yet nothing in particular.

They took pictures of themselves in the back of the cab and sent them to one another trying to hang on to every moment they could, knowing this would be the last time they would see each other for a long time.

While at the museum, Jessica reluctantly began to contemplate the idea of her friend moving all the way to Texas and moving in with complete strangers. Not knowing how or when to bring up this touchy subject, Jessica decided it best to just put it out there and let the chips fall where they may. After all, she had Celina's best interest in mind and didn't want her friend to be setting herself up for failure or disappointment.

After an hour or so of inwardly debating how she was going to bring the matter up, Jessica suggested that they go to the museum's restaurant called "The Modern" to have a drink or two.

Celina not knowing her friend's hidden agenda happily agreed, but insisted that only if she could pay. They made their way to the restaurant and once they were inside, Jessica looked around for a minute and found a table away from everyone so they could speak freely and without interruption. They ordered a glass of white wine and sat there for a moment in uncomfortable silence. Celina could sense something out of the ordinary was troubling her friend.

"So what was on your mind, Jessie?"

Jessica took a deep breath and replied, "Look, it's not that I don't want to be supportive of your decision or anything, I'm just wondering how much thought you've really put in to all this."

"Like what do you mean?" Celina asked.

"Oh, my God! Okay, for starters, how well do you really know these people? How do you know they can be trusted? Are you fucking him or something?"

"No I'm not fucking him. Not yet anyway," Celina said jokingly.

"Look, stop playing. I'm not kidding. I'm being serious," Jessica said. She was now feeling even more concerned that Celina might be making a huge mistake.

Jessica took a deep breath and said, "Tell me the truth, Celina; you're not moving over there so you can be closer to Jaime are you? I know your still writing to him."

Feeling the lack of trust Jessica had in her decision, Celina said to her, "All right, look, please try and understand. I'm looking at this as an opportunity to expand on my love for the Southwest when it comes to my artwork. Not to be closer to Jaime." Then she redirected Jessica's thoughts.

"Besides, I haven't written to him in weeks. Whatever hold you may think he has over me is not stronger than my will to succeed. Come on, think about almost all of the pieces I've made over the years. They all have a southwestern flair. Fernando's gallery is in the heart of the Southwest. He is a respectable man in the business who saw something in me that no one else has. I am not just jumping into something I know I can't handle. Besides it would be different if he weren't established. Plus he's married, and I spoke to his wife today, and she seemed really nice, too. I know what I'm doing."

Jessica sat there sipping on her glass of wine trying to soak in all that was being said and play it over in her head to find any reason why Celina shouldn't go. But the more she thought about it, the more she began to realize that Celina might be right. Celina began to explain that maybe one of the reasons why people weren't buying much of her work up here in New York was because of their lack of appreciation for her kind of work.

Just then Celina received a text letting her know that she had new e-mail in her inbox. Celina went online and opened up her e-mail to find that Paulina just sent her plane ticket along with a short message.

She looked up at Jessica and told her, "You see? They just sent me my ticket. Hang on, let me read what it says."

"Please find enclosed your plane ticket from New York La Guardia Airport to Dallas Fort Worth International. I will pick you up on Tuesday when you arrive at 3:00 PM at gate 2B. Please keep in mind you are under no obligation to redeem these tickets, but if you decide you no longer wish to come, a courtesy call would be appreciated. The tickets are also refundable and open ended in the event you decide to go back at any time. If you have any questions or concerns, please feel free to reach me at 817-555-2345, Paulina."

"You see, I told you they were good people."

In a last ditch effort to make a dent in Celina's stubborn mind, Jessica asked her to reiterate how she met Fernando.

Celina said with a smile, "Andy introduced us the other night at my last showing in the Village."

"Oh great, Andy," she said sarcastically. "Yeah, that's better," she proclaimed.

"What's that supposed to mean?"

"Well, come on! Andy! Really?"

Celina became offended. Her best friend was making it seem as though she didn't already know what kind of man Andy was, or that she couldn't make good choices without Jessica's input.

"Look, I thought you of all people would be more understanding." Then she muttered, "I need to go home and pack."

Celina made her way to the bar to pay for their drinks leaving Jessica behind to think about everything they had said.

Jessica went over to Celina, took her by the hand and said, "I'm sorry, sweetie. You know I love you. I just don't want to see you get hurt. You're my best friend, and I just want to make sure you'll be okay. That's all."

"I know, Jessie. I'm scared, too," she said. They hugged and began to wipe the tears in their eyes and simultaneously pulled out their mirrors from their handbags to check their makeup. The feeling of loss was becoming heavier, but Celina pushed it to the back of her mind.

"Now come back with me to my place and help me pack."

CHAPTER FIVE

They Prepare To Meet

That afternoon, Fernando was taking inventory at the gallery. He took his clipboard and walked the gallery, checking off every piece he'd printed out. His receptionist, Christie, was completing transactions and writing up delivery tickets for the twins, Eric and Alex.

They were identical twins and were young, handsome and hard working. Fernando's mother had been acquainted with their mother in Mexico, and after learning of their arrival in Texas, she referred them to Fernando for work. Fernando helped them get their CDL licensing and provided them with enough funds to secure an apartment close to the gallery. The twins were extremely loyal to Fernando and Paulina because of that generosity.

Just then, five people came into the gallery and began surveying the art on display.

"Welcome to De La Mar Gallery," he announced.

Fernando took note of the type of vehicles they drove, their clothing, and the way they carried themselves as they perused his gallery. He was a skilled salesman, but he allowed them a few minutes to take in the length of the building before approaching them to ask if they had any questions. He knew the fundamental rule of sales was, of course, to sell himself first.

"I'm Fernando De La Mar. Are ya'll from around here?"

"No," the eldest of the group replied. "We're from Santa Fe. We're just visiting our son Michael over there who lives here in Fort Worth."

"Oh, that's great," he said. "I've lived here all my life," he began to explain. "I opened this place about seven years ago with my wife who should be here any minute now as a matter of fact. So anyway, make yourselves at home and I'll send my assistant Christie over here in a little while to check on you, okay?"

"Sounds great," the gentleman said. "Thank you."

Fernando glanced out the front window, saw that Paulina had pulled in, and began to make his way to the back to greet her. He stopped behind the counter to whisper in Christie's ear as she was filling out some paperwork from her previous transaction to make sure she periodically checked in on their guests.

"Yes, sir," she replied flirtatiously. "Whatever you like, you're the boss." He shrugged off her ridiculous overture, and began to make his way to the back to open the garage door for Paulina.

"What possessed you to drive the Rover today? You never drive the Rover."

"Yeah, I know I hate driving it, but I stopped by to pick up some office supplies we needed. Can you have one of the guys bring it inside?" she asked.

"Yeah, sure," he said.

Fernando tossed the keys to Alex and asked if he would put everything up for him in the storage room. They went inside through the warehouse, and Paulina immediately began to complain to Eric to pick up all the boxes they had thrown all over the floor.

Paulina was asking Fernando how he could allow them to be so messy when Fernando told her they just had some new pieces shipped to them that morning. He asked her if everything was okay.

She said she was fine but just a little frustrated from trying to get all of the travel arrangements squared away for Celina's arrival.

"She seems like a nice girl," she told Fernando as she sat down in his antique leather chair. "I just hope she's worth all the trouble."

"Yeah, me too," he agreed. "I just don't want you to worry, babe. I'm a pretty good judge of character, and I wouldn't have made her that offer if it was going to cause any problems."

"No, it's not that," she said. "But I just wonder what my parents will think once they find out."

"Well, we just won't say anything for a while—or at least until we know she's going to work out," he said.

"Anyway what did she say when you called her?" he asked.

They Prepare To Meet

"Not much. I think we were both a little nervous at first, then she began to tell me how she met Andy. Now that was funny," she said.

"Oh yeah, that's right. Andy told me how he tried to get her. What a jerk," he said of his friend.

"So, anyway, what's the plan? When is she coming down?" he asked.

"She should be here tomorrow at three o'clock." She said nonchalantly.

"Tomorrow at three o'clock? Oh, shit! I didn't think she would be here that quick!" he exclaimed. "I need to get home."

"For what?" she asked.

"I need to make sure the guesthouse is ready."

"Just send one of the guys in the morning," she said. "Let one of them straighten it up."

"I guess," he said knowing he was overreacting.

"So who are those people in the gallery?" she asked as she looked out his office window.

"They're just some people from out of town."

"Well, I'm going to go say hello to them and see if they need any help since no one else is assisting them."

"Okay," he said. "Well, just the same I'm going to call it a day so I can make sure everything is ready back at home."

"All right, all right," she said, noting how unusually excited he was about this woman.

Fernando got up and said, "Okay, hon. I'll see you at home. Love you."

Paulina ignored him and walked out to the gallery floor. She strategically went up to one of the ladies and began making small talk, while casting Christie a dark look. Paulina never liked Christie that much and knew that she would frequently make passes at her husband when she wasn't around. She often criticized Fernando for keeping her around as long as he had, but Fernando insisted on giving her chance after chance saying that she was a nice girl and that she was good for appealing to a younger crowd.

Paulina didn't take long to charm her way into making a sale to the visitors by offering free shipment to them if they were to make a purchase that day.

Paulina instructed Christie (who was busy texting one of her friends on her cell phone) to wrap up the order with them and advised her that she would be heading out soon.

Paulina walked back into Fernando's office to get her keys, and she suddenly remembered that she needed to update their shipping books. Everything was updated within five minutes when it occurred to her to "Google" Celina.

She debated on whether or not that kind of behavior would be considered stalking, but then before she could stop herself, she typed in her name.

There were thousands of records for a Celina Santa Cruz online. She scrolled through the various selections trying to find one of interest, but ended up clicking the first one she came across. She was able to see for herself some of Celina's artwork and read some of the articles on her. Before she knew it, she came across a few pictures of the artist herself. A young vivacious Celina was portrayed at her home in New York working on a sculpture of some sort.

Paulina was so taken back at her beauty that she herself was lost in thought. The only thing she could think of was how much she hoped that her husband's intentions with this young woman were strictly business-related. She wondered if she should back out of this deal before it was too late.

Paulina also considered the thought that having someone like Celina around might be a challenge to both her and her husband. They would see if they could stay true to each other, even if it meant losing one another.

Fighting the afternoon traffic, Paulina left the gallery and began the long drive home to their house near Benbrook Lake. She fidgeted with her car radio, trying to find some music that would calm her nerves and help her forget the images that were burned in her mind. The sound of her mother's disapproving voice overpowered the song on the radio.

"How can you let some woman live in your home that neither one of you know? What are you thinking?"

Paulina knew her mother was extremely old-fashioned, but reminded herself that it was her mother who kept her father's temper in check, for the most part. Paulina loved and trusted Fernando even though their romantic life had changed over the years. She had tried to spice up their love life by wearing sexy lingerie for him and even buying adult novelties and movies on the Internet. But nothing she ever did could quite satisfy the feeling that something was definitely missing.

She recalled an evening of too much alcohol when she had foolishly asked Fernando what his secret sexual fantasy was. But Fernando just laughed at her questions and changed the subject. She made up her mind that she would bring it up to him again.

Once home, she picked out a bottle of wine to chill for later that evening. She decided to prepare the bedroom for an evening of romance. She walked over to the dresser to rummage for something to wear, and she could see through the window that the lights were on in the guesthouse.

She sat down on the bed, closed her eyes, and thought to herself if it was worth all the trouble to go through with what she had planned. Paulina walked back to the mirror to check her appearance and began to notice things that were more clear to her than any other day before.

She noticed strands of gray had appeared in her hair and had mixed in with her natural auburn shade. There were small lines on her face—mostly around her honey-colored eyes—and even wrinkles on her long slim hands. She lifted her breasts and turned around to see what damage gravity had done to her bottom.

Paulina had been a cheerleader throughout high school and won several medals in track and field. She worked out three days a week in their home gym and pool. She was in the best physical shape she could possibly be in—for her age.

"For my age," she said out loud, letting the words sink in. She was no longer that pretty, high school cheerleader that had the entire roster of male students chasing after her. She was no longer the carefree, naïve and lovesick young woman that defied her parents to marry the man they didn't approve of. She had spent the last twelve years of her life with that man who, as she stared sadly at herself in her closet mirror, was happily making their guesthouse some sort of love nest for his new protégé.

Paulina swallowed hard and sat back down hard on the bed, trying to make sense of it all.

Despite the occasional flirtations that had come her way during her marriage, Fernando was the only one she ever wanted to impress. She felt a sinking feeling of desperation over everything she was doing to try and re-kindle their love life but decided it was best to stay the course. Knowing that Anita normally set the table for dinner around seven o'clock, she elected to freshen up and decide what to wear later.

Fernando on the other hand was making ready the guesthouse, moving things around, and making sure the basic essentials were all intact. They would often have guests come in from out of town as they were both from big families and sometimes held overnight parties with friends who were just too drunk to drive home after one of his famous poker nights.

It was for this reason they had fixed up what used to be a pool house in the back yard. It was used mostly for extra storage, but a couple months earlier they had donated a lot of things to charity.

All he had left to do was wipe down the counters, check the light bulbs, sweep the floors, and a few more things of that nature. He looked around one more time before calling it quits, wishing he had more time to prepare for his new guest. Not having anything left to do, he turned off the lights, locked the doors behind him, and headed back to the house.

When he walked inside he could hear the radio playing in the kitchen and could smell the tasty aromas coming from Anita's cooking.

He went to go see what Anita was making, and she immediately told him she was making arroz con pollo, one of his favorite dishes. He grabbed a beer, went into the den, and turned on the TV to watch the news.

He began to doze off when Anita cried out, "Dinner is ready!"

He woke up startled to find Paulina standing in the doorway, fresh out of the shower in a bathrobe.

"Wake up, honey, it's time to eat," she said in a soft voice.

"Okay," he said still trying to fight the sleep in his eyes. "I'll be there in a minute."

After washing his face, he walked to the dining room where Paulina was lighting the candles in the middle of the table. With a confused look on his face, he asked what she was up to.

"Why are you lighting the candles?" he asked. "You never light those candles."

"I don't know," she replied. "I just thought I would do something different for a change. Sit down, babe, and let me get you some wine."

Liking the attention she was giving him, he did as he was told and sat there quietly allowing her to take control. Fernando always admired how Paulina could sometimes be demanding. He found the way she was speaking to him somewhat arousing even though he did not know where it was coming from.

Paulina went over to Anita, who was busy cleaning the dishes and said to her, "You can go now, Anita. I've got it from here."

"Okay, Paulina, don't forget to tell Fernando I picked up his clothes from the cleaners today and put them away in the closet."

"Okay," Paulina answered. "By the way, you can have the day off tomorrow, too."

"Really?" Anita asked.

"Yes. We are having company tomorrow, and we will be taking her out to dinner."

Paulina took out the bottle of wine she had chilling in the refrigerator and grabbed the bottle opener to take to Fernando. By the time she went back to the den, Fernando had almost finished eating. She handed him the bottle opener and almost lost her composure when she saw he had begun to eat without her. But she blew it off, reminding herself that he didn't mean any harm. Besides it's not like she told him of her dastardly plan.

He looked at the particular label she had selected, and that's when it dawned on him that he may have forgotten about a special occasion or something. He opened the wine, poured them a glass, and began to change his demeanor. But instead of burning countless brain cells trying to figure out what she already seemed to know, he simply asked her.

"So, what's the occasion?"

"Nothing," she said innocently. "Can't I seduce my husband every once in a while?"

Relieved that he hadn't missed a birthday or anniversary or something, he replied, "Oh, of course. Don't get me wrong, I like what you're doing. It's rather nice. We haven't done this in a long while."

They both began to look at each other not saying a word. Fernando reached out to brush his hand against her cheek. They began to kiss passionately, rubbing and touching as they made their way upstairs. A line of garments draped the stairs as they peeled the clothes off each other. The room was already lit with vanilla-scented candles that Paulina had lit earlier.

She felt the warmth of his manhood enter her slowly as she began to moan. As she released the tingling between her legs, he knew he had reached a part of her spirit that only he knew how. Then, in the middle of intercourse, she surprised him. She wanted to role-play with him.

"Pretend I'm someone else," she whispered.

"Like whom?" he asked carefully.

"I don't know," she giggled. "How about that girl you met in New York."

"Celina?" suddenly he could feel himself become even more aroused.

"Yes," she said confidently. "Pretend I'm her. Show me what you would do to her if she were here."

His thrusts became deeper, and she loved every minute of it. She asked him to call her "Celina" as he made love to her. He closed his eyes and imagined Celina lying in front of him. With her eyes closed, she imagined what it would be like to share her husband with another woman and orchestrated from there.

They had never done anything like that before. It was both steamy and spontaneous, not to mention one of the most erotic experiences they had ever shared. After an hour of sharing each other, they lay there trying to catch their breath in exhaustion. She snuggled him closer, wrapping her legs around his with her head resting on his chest.

"How did you like it, baby?" she asked lovingly. "Did that turn you on?"

Carefully he admitted, "Yeah, it was great. What got in to you?"

"I don't know," she wondered. "I just thought you might like role playing for a change. Do you think I'm weird?

"No, quite the opposite," he assured her. "I think it's healthy for a man and woman who love each other to be creative like that every once in a while." Then he asked her a very delicate question and didn't quite know how she would respond. He curiously asked, "Do you think you could ever watch me with another woman?"

Her reaction surprised him yet again. Instead of getting upset or smashing the lamp over his head, she rolled over and said "Yeah. I think I could. I think it would be hot."

His mouth nearly dropped. He tried to replay what she had just said. He couldn't believe that his sweet, innocent wife was more daring and naughty than he had known. It was hard for him to accept this side of her.

He rolled over to look her in the eye and said, "Yeah, right. You mean to tell me that you could honestly lay there and watch me make love to another woman and not feel jealous?"

"Well," she said absorbing the idea. "Yes. I think that perhaps in the beginning I would be a little jealous. I mean, what woman wouldn't? I guess it just depends on what our intentions were—that would make the difference."

He was puzzled to hear her talk that way. But he allowed her to continue.

"Okay. look, if we were to hire an escort to spice up things a bit, of course I would not be jealous at all. She would be there just to fill that purpose, and that's all. But, if you were to have an affair with another woman behind my back, and I walked in on ya'll, of course things would be a lot different. You wouldn't have to worry about me being jealous, you would have to worry about me cutting it off, if you know what I mean." He gasped.

"But, if we were to agree to bringing someone into our lives that we could both love, that might be different. And I don't mean love like sexually on my part, but love and care for like a sister."

"You could do that?" he doubted.

"Why not?" she fired back. "I'm mature enough to know that you wouldn't leave me. And I would much rather we do something like that than to take a chance of you cheating on me. Whenever I hear about the rate of divorce throughout the country, it scares me to think of ever divorcing you and losing everything we have. If people were smart enough, why couldn't they reach an understanding when it comes to something like that? We make compromises with everything else, right? I think it's somewhat shallow for someone to think they are the only person another person could love. Haven't you ever met someone and thought to yourself what it might be like if you were with them instead of someone you were with at the time?"

"No. Why, have you?" he said convincingly.

"Well, yeah. I think most everyone does at some point. The difference is that most women won't act on it. But I think men do act more often, because it's a part of their natural instinct. Take Celina for example. I'm sure she is a very attractive and interesting person who may have a lot to offer. Why wouldn't you fall for someone like that? Honestly? Hypothetically, what if I said I would be okay with you starting a relationship with her?"

"You could do that?" he asked.

She replied, "Well, no. Not now. I don't even know her. But if I found that she was fit for you, and she was open minded—it could work. She would have to be worthy of something of this magnitude and would have to be respectful, but I…"

He interrupted her in an attempt to find out how they even got on this topic. "Wait, babe. Where is all this coming from?" he asked.

"Just forget it," she said as she pulled the blankets over her head. She closed her eyes and drifted off into sleep. Fernando was left contemplating what they had talked about and tossing and turning before falling asleep himself.

CHAPTER SIX

Celina Becomes a Texan

Celina and Jessica had packed just enough clothes to last through the end of the week when they said their goodbyes. They had bonded more than ever before in their last hours together—talking about their ups and downs, good times and bad, and what they had meant to each other over the years.

Celina was not very sentimental, but as the realization of leaving set in, she couldn't help but allow her tears to flow. Jessica, on the other hand, didn't shed any tears as she was trying to stay strong for her friend. The last words Celina told Jessica was that she hated goodbyes, and that she would see her in the near future.

Now alone in the house for what seemed to be an eternity until dawn, Celina kicked off her shoes, lay on her bed exhausted, and tried to fall asleep.

Celina tossed and turned all night replaying the decision that moving to Texas would be the right decision for her. But in the end, the more she thought about it the more she knew she was making the right choice.

The thought of being that much closer to her dreams had kept her from her sleep, however. She kept waking up after dreaming of one day owning her own gallery where she could sell her own works and live the life she had always dreamed of. She recalled when she was younger how hard it had been for her mother to keep afloat sometimes.

After coming to America, her mother always had to work two jobs, and sometimes three, just to make it; she didn't get to spend a lot of time with her daughter. She had to leave Celina in the hands of day care centers, schools and friends until Celina was around twelve years old. Celina always seemed to do well in school, even though her upbringing was tough living in such rough conditions.

Her passion for the arts also began at the age of twelve when she took a field trip to the Metropolitan Museum and attended a free seminar where they encouraged young students to express themselves freely. Her vivid imagination and creativity would flow through any canvas she brushed across and immediately caught the attention of fellow art lovers at the museum.

Doing well in school had also paid off to the point that people who worked at her school and the museum, pulled money together and bought her a first set of paint brushes, easel and blank canvasses. From there, history would write the rest of the story.

Still awake, Celina, went into the living room to watch late night TV and clinched a pillow she had made out of down feathers and cotton. After a couple of hours, she finally rested in peaceful sleep. Just like raindrops hitting a tin roof can put someone to sleep, the sound of elevated subways cars and horns blowing from the taxicabs below had put Celina at rest.

A few hours passed, and she was awakened to the sound of distant music coming from her alarm clock in the bedroom, where she had was set it for earlier than usual. That, along with the aroma of freshly brewed coffee from Mrs. Fuentes apartment upstairs and the sounds of little children in the hallway running off to school, gave her a last impression of living in the city.

She got up and headed straight to the kitchen to use up the last bit of the Southern Pecan coffee she had bought days before, reminding her of the southern gentleman who was to be the biggest influence in her life up to that point.

Allowing the coffee to brew, she brought out some of her mother's old teacups she had left behind before she died. Those teacups were the only connection between her mother and her childhood. Celina held one of the cups which had no other value than her own attachment to it and wondered if her mother would be proud of the woman she was becoming.

Two sugars and a splash of milk later, Celina sat near a window overlooking an alley in the rear of her apartment. After savoring every drop, she decided to take a warm bath and turned up the music that was coming from the bedroom.

She undressed and hung her robe on the door behind her. She came across some bath beads that she had purchased for herself for Christmas the year before and thought there was no better time than the present to use them. The smell of lavender filled the air as the hot water began to fog up the mirror. A bath like this one was just what the doctor ordered; she lay there in makeshift tranquility.

She debated how to spend her final moments before her 1,500-mile journey, but only two things were coming to mind. Should I stay home and catch up on my soaps or should I take pencil to paper, go to Central Park, and sketch? Deciding on the latter, she dried herself off and got ready to head out to the park.

Celina was the type of woman who didn't need to spend time putting on lots of makeup and fixing her hair, she was the envy of most women when it came to showing off her natural beauty. As she made her way there, she was having a hard time choosing which part of the park to visit; she had an overwhelming desire to see, one last time, one of her favorite sculptures, "Indian Hunter," as it's known. It was the first sculpture in Central Park by an American artist and was placed in the park in 1869.

She sat down on a bench nearby and took out her sketchbook and pencil sharpener only to be bothered by two young men taking a morning jog. The joggers who were running towards her apparently noticed that Celina sat alone.

They began to jog in place in front her until one of them said, "Hey beautiful, do you mind if we join you?" Annoyed, she replied "Sorry, but I don't think my husband would like that much. Now, if you don't mind, I'd like to finish my sketch."

The nice gentlemen started to run off when one of them whispered to the other, "What a bitch!" showing the ass he truly was for not having the decency to respect a woman's privacy.

Just the same Celina did not allow that to deter her from why she was there. Sketching the birds drinking from pools of water on the ground, passerbys, and mothers as they pushed their babies in their strollers, just wasn't doing for her what she had previously envisioned.

She closed her eyes and drifted off to Texas where she envisioned what the house she would be living in would look like. She pictured a two-story, wood framed house with a white picket fence nestled a half mile off a dirt road. Laughing to herself and knowing that was probably not the case, she realized what little she knew of Fernando.

She began to picture what Paulina would look like. Replaying the voice she had heard over the phone, she imagined a tall skinny white woman in her thirties with big red hair, blue eyes and too much makeup. A trophy wife, as they are called.

She started sketching the image she had in her mind while wishing to herself that Fernando would have told her on the night they met that he was married. Forgiving him almost immediately, she sat there in concentration and blocked out all the sounds in the background to finish her drawing.

A text message interrupted her a few moments later, and she hurried as she pulled her phone out of her bag. It was Paulina.

"Hi, Celina, its Paulina," it read. "Text me once you arrive at DFW and I will take you from there. See you soon."

Excited to read what Paulina wrote, she started then erased a couple of responses before she replied with a single sentence: "Okay, will do!"

She rushed home to change and to make sure she watered the plants and locked up before she left. It didn't take long before she was back in her apartment where her luggage was waiting for her by the door. She grabbed her things, and as she headed outside, she thought how funny it was how she didn't waste any time senselessly looking around to take in one more view of the apartment she had kept for nearly three years.

Taking the stairs instead of the elevator, she ran into her neighbors, the O'Donnell's, an elderly Irish couple who lived next door, who asked her where she was going to in such a hurry. Not wanting to lie or spend what she knew would be a lot of time with them, she said she was taking a trip to Texas about a job offer she had.

"Oh, is that right?" Mrs. O'Donnell said. "Will you be moving then?"

"Yes, I might be," she said over her shoulder, never actually stopping to talk to them.

"We'll be wishing you luck then…"

Celina simply waved goodbye to her neighbors as she made her way down the stairs carrying her three bags of luggage, mostly clothes that should last her about two to three weeks. Once downstairs and onto the sidewalk, Celina hailed a cab and said to the driver "La Guardia, please", and off she went.

It was around an hour before her flight left when she got to the airport. She checked two bags and was carrying on the one that had her personal effects including her laptop on which she planned to watch a movie. Her stomach began to feel empty as she remembered that she hadn't eaten breakfast, or it could have been butterflies due to her nerves.

Either way she took a short walk around the airport and saw a sign that said "Five Dollar New York Style Pizza just outside Terminal D." Of course, not knowing when she would get another chance to eat *real* New York pizza again, she could not pass up that opportunity, even if it was at the airport.

"Oh, My God...this is so good! Damn, it's things like this that I'm going to miss the most," she thought as she took another bite of her folded pie. "I guess I'll have to fall in love with Texas barbeque going forward," she thought to herself and grinned.

Picking up a paper someone had left on the table, she began to settle her nerves and continue in her self-indulgence-by clearing her mind of any other details of her day.

"Now boarding, Flight 1177 to DFW" came over the loud speakers and you could almost feel the excitement that overcame Celina as she put down her paper and threw away her plate.

She made the short walk towards the gate to stand in line and take her seat in no time. That's when she noticed her tickets were in first class. Seeing that didn't help her nerves any, because she had never flown first class before.

"Great," she said to herself. "I should have known." Not much time went by before she found herself in the plane sitting in a leather seat next to the window with all the other people in first class.

She whispered to herself, "So this is what first class feels like. There's no turning back now." In no time, she was in the air and Texas bound.

Three-and-a-half hours later, she looked out the window and saw the city skyline of the Big D as she arrived at DFW International Airport right on time. As the plane made its way to the gate, she reached for her cell phone to see a text from Jessica.

"Have a safe trip, and don't forget to call me." She smiled as she began a reply then remembered her first priority.

"Oh, shit! I have to tell Paulina I'm here." She immediately texted Paulina to tell her she had landed and what she was wearing so that there would be no mistaking her.

Paulina replied, "LOL. Okay, I'll be on the lookout for you."

Knowing she would be one of the first people to exit the plane, she hated the fact that she didn't know what to expect of Paulina. She slowly made her way out of the plane trying to notice anyone who made eye contact with her.

Not seeing anyone right away, she turned to a set of blue chairs grouped together just outside of the gate to put down her bag.

Just then she felt a tap on her shoulder. As she turned to greet her assailant, she was stunned speechless for a moment.

"Celina?" A tall, very fashionably dressed woman was smiling at her. Celina was staring into the prettiest hazel green eyes she had ever seen. Thick, dark lashes fringed the woman's almond-shaped eyes beautifully, and her facial structure was symmetrically perfect with high cheekbones and full, pouty lips.

"Hi. You must be Paulina?" she smiled nervously and extended her hand, trying not to stare.

"That's me! It's very nice to meet you finally," Paulina took Celina's hand gently, equally struck by the younger woman's beauty.

"So how was your trip?"

"It was good, thanks. I've never flown first class before," she admitted shyly.

"Yeah, Fernando travels a lot so we get great deals all the time. I can't begin to tell you how many frequent flier miles he's racked up. Did you bring more luggage?"

"Yes, I did. I just have to pick them up, and then we can be on our way," Celina said, eagerly looking around for the baggage claim area.

"It's this way," Paulina smiled, recognizing the look on Celina's face. "Come on. I'll help you."

They made their way through the airport feeling a little awkward and not saying too much to each other. Eventually, Celina grabbed the rest of her luggage, and they made their way to Paulina's' new Mercedes. Celina never had a car while living in New York. Everywhere she went she took a cab, got on the subway or hitched a ride with friends.

"Wow I like your car," she said admiringly.

"Oh, Thanks. Ferny doesn't seem to like it much. He said it's too bourgeois for his taste."

"Oh, really?" she replied. "What does he drive?"

"He drives a Land Rover, but he mostly rides the horse to work...just kidding!" she said trying to break the ice. "I know that's what most people think of people who live in Texas."

"For a second, I thought you were serious!" Celina giggled.

For some reason, they quickly began to feel a sense of compatibility as they conversed with one another. Celina was very talkative, telling Paulina everything she went through leading up to that point. She told her how she was looking forward to making a fresh start.

Paulina nodded her head in agreement as she listened to her tell her side of her story. Never once did she give Celina an idea of how she too felt reluctant in the beginning to have someone come to live in her house.

"So, where are we headed first?" Celina asked.

"Well, I thought I would take you to see the gallery so you can see it for yourself. From there, I'll take you to the house so you can get settled in before we go out to eat. Fernando is there waiting for us back at the gallery," she replied. "I took him to work today so that we could all ride home together."

"Oh, that's cool," Celina said.

They made their way up HWY 183 towards Fort Worth, zooming in and out of DFW afternoon traffic. Celina held on tight as Paulina was never one to drive slowly. They exited Henderson off Interstate 30 into downtown, turned left on West7th Street and pulled into De La Mar Gallery.

"So, are you nervous? Paulina asked Celina as they pulled in to the parking lot.

"A little bit, but I think I'm more excited than nervous, to tell you the truth."

"By the way," she added as Paulina turned the engine off, "I just wanted to say again how much I appreciate everything. I know it may not have been easy especially for you to agree to all this. But I just want you to know that I would never do anything to interrupt you or your husband's life in any way. But promise me something,... If I do or say anything that makes you feel uncomfortable, please tell me right away. I won't know I'm doing something wrong if you don't tell me okay?"

Paulina sat there in awe listening to every word Celina had to say. She was about to speak when Celina continued. "Look, for what it's worth, I am pretty much a loner. I didn't have very many friends when I lived in New York. I pretty much just stayed to myself in my apartment working on something or trying to find a place to sell or show my stuff. I sold a lot of my work on the Internet or by word of mouth. So you won't have to worry about me too much when it comes to getting in your hair" she said laughingly.

"But honestly, I wish my mom was around or that I had a big sister to share my new venture with. I told my friends but it's not the same."

Seeing that statement as her opportunity to let her know her own reservations about the whole thing, Paulina looked at Celina and said, "Look, you seem like a really nice person, and I don't see anything wrong with you being here. I, we, for that matter, want you to feel at home. I know this is quite a big move for you and I want you to feel welcome. There is nothing worse than walking on eggshells around people you hardly know. So believe me, I understand where you're coming from. But I appreciate your honesty. Now come on, let's go inside. I'm sure he probably noticed us pull in by now and if I know Fernando, he's probably wondering what the heck is going on," she said jokingly.

Fernando did notice them as they pulled up and sat in the car for what seemed like an eternity. He began to sweat as he paced back and forth not knowing if he should go outside and check on them or send his wife a text. He didn't know what to do. But he remained as calm as possible fearing the worst of the unknown.

His nerves settled as they made their way to the front door. Then he pretended to walk from the rear of the building as Paulina opened the door for Celina.

"Hi, come on in," he said as he walked towards them giving Paulina a kiss on the cheek.

"Welcome to De La Mar Gallery," he said to Celina extending his hand. "How was your trip?"

"It was fine," Celina said with her eyes wide open. I can't believe I'm here," she said as she shook his hand.

"Can I get you something to drink, some water or a soda? We have some wine, too, if you'd like."

"No, I'm fine, thanks. So this is your place?" she said as she took a quick glance around. "I like it. It's so… Fort Worth!" they all laughed.

Fernando suggested to Paulina to show Celina around while he went to tell Christie they would be leaving soon. He excused himself as he went to go lock up his office and told Christie to call him if she needed any help.

The twins also came out front so take a peek at what was going on because they overheard of this mysterious woman the day before when Christie was telling one of her friends over the phone.

Fernando also asked Eric, the more responsible one of the two, if he could come in tomorrow a little early to assist Christie up front with customers and such. Eric kindly agreed having helped out in the past whenever Fernando and Paulina went on vacations and things of that nature.

Fernando quietly went up to the girls and asked, "Are ya'll ready?"

"Yes. Is everything okay?" Paulina asked Fernando.

"Yeah, I just had to make sure everybody was okay first. By the way, just so you know, I asked Eric to watch the store tomorrow so we don't have to come in. I thought it would be nice to show Celina around town."

Celina smiled big as Paulina replied, "Oh, that's a good idea. That's what I love about Fern, he always thinks of everything," she told Celina.

Now feeling a little more at ease about the whole thing, Paulina also began to get excited thinking of all the things around town that they could show Celina. She began to think of things they could do the next day.

Her inner emotions were actually thoughts of spending the day alongside her husband. Paulina's love language from Fernando was the time he would spend with her. She didn't look at it so much as time they would be spending time with someone else, but rather the time she could spend with him and show someone else something they both loved.

"Well, let's head out" he said. "Would you like me to drive honey?"

"Yes baby, I don't feel like driving." Paulina said in a loving manner as she stole a kiss from him.

Celina could feel the love they had for one another thinking what a sweet couple they made wishing she had someone in her life that she could share those kind of moments with. She thought briefly of Jaime and how he never considered her feelings or desires.

They got in the car and pressed on but about half way there it dawned on Celina to ask a question that just she had not asked before.

"So how many kids do you guys have?"

Fernando and Paulina looked at each other before Paulina let out a sigh and replied, "We don't have any kids."

"Oh?" Celina said somewhat surprised. "I thought you guys would have two or three kids running around. Why not? If you don't mind me asking."

Paulina slightly turned in her seat and began to explain to her that it wasn't for a lack of trying and how they wish they did have children. She told her that it was not due to any condition or because they didn't want any children but for some reason they have yet to be blessed in that way.

Celina listened to Paulina explain to her why they didn't have any children, and asked if they ever thought about adopting and how she thought they would make great parents. But Celina picked up that this was too touchy a subject and did not want to press the issue.

She almost felt sad for them how unfair it was for two people who loved each other as much as they did would never have life beyond their own. She just sat there in the back seat not speaking too much just taking in the majestic countryside of north Texas.

The view began to change as they drove into their estate. It was a beautiful two-story southwestern style hacienda sitting on a hill with a large remote-controlled cast iron and stone gate that wrapped the entrance. Long Branch Ranch was a five- bedroom, four-and-one-half bath gracious Texas home with a four-car garage that sat on about five acres of land. It had rows of pecan trees throughout the property that provided shade to the white graveled driveway and the well-manicured lawn of green grass. The lawn would tempt anyone to run on it barefooted.

The look on Celina's face was priceless as they drove closer and closer to the house. It was nothing like she had imagined.

"Welcome to The Long Branch Ranch," Fernando said casually as he parked the car.

"I hate when you call it that," Paulina said rolling her eyes.

"Don't mind him. He says that every time we bring someone new to the house."

"Hey, leave me alone you know I like calling it that. Why don't ya'll go inside, and I'll grab the luggage?"

"Come on, Celina let's have the cowboy get your stuff and I'll show you around inside."

Just then, a set of full-grown Akitas came to greet them. Celina yelped in surprised and took a few steps back.

Fernando laughed at her reaction and said, "These are our dogs Mop and Bucket." Mop was the female and Bucket was the male. Both were very friendly as they wagged their tails at Celina.

Fernando had given the pups to Paulina for Christmas 3 years ago after she had spotted them in a little flea market just south of the city. Seeing how the pups lit up Paulina's face when she first saw them, he made it a point to go back and buy them for her a few days later and asked the people if they could keep them for him until closer to Christmas. Once it was time to go and get them, he placed the puppies in a kennel and gift wrapped three sides of it with wrapping paper.

After opening up all her gifts that Christmas morning, he took Paulina into another room of the house and asked her to unveil what he had given her. To her surprise it was the same exact puppies she had saw just 3 weeks before and they had been with them ever since.

Celina and Paulina went inside and Paulina began showing Celina the inside of their luxurious home while Fernando took Celina's belongings to the guest house. He placed them inside the guest house taking one final look around to make sure he didn't forget anything, then closed the door behind him and walked to the main house. Entering the back door, he overheard Celina asking which one of them was the decorator. He interrupted by saying "I am," as he walked through the kitchen and into the living room.

A look of amazement came over Celina as Paulina reluctantly agreed. The house had more of a Texas theme to it with its rustic-style furniture and a huge deer head trophy that hung over the stone fireplace. Although Fernando was an avid hunter, Paulina would only allow that one trophy of his in the house. Most of them were in the garage, and one was conveniently displayed at his office at the gallery.

Although the majority of the house was decorated by him, Paulina did manage to decorate the kitchen where she spent most of her time and of course the master bedroom because there was no way she would give him that much freedom over that intimate part of their home.

Celina could not help but laugh as she agreed with Paulina that a woman should never allow a man that much control over the couple's home decoration.

After giving Celina the grand tour, Paulina and Fernando asked her if she was ready to see the guesthouse where she would be staying.

They walked her through the back yard and passed the pool where they also showed her the outdoor hot tub and patio wet bar. Fernando told Celina how they would occasionally host poker parties with a few friends outside on the patio and how he loved cooking on the barbeque grill for them whenever he could.

All this was a bit of a culture shock to Celina. She had never lived in such a huge place, never had dogs, never had a pool, and never had homemade barbeque. The lifestyle of this couple was something she had only read about or seen on TV.

Fernando handed Celina a set of keys, and Celina nervously opened the door. She took a few minutes to survey the place, going in the kitchen, checking the bedroom then heading back to the living area. Every footfall created an echo because of the emptiness of the room. The smell of freshly painted white walls and the ammonia Fernando had used to clean up the room was intense.

The walls were plain, and the room had very little furniture, so Celina couldn't help but feel that something was missing. Fernando reminded her that if she did decide to stay, she should imagine it with all of her own belongings.

Celina explained shyly that the room's lack of furnishings was not the problem. She thought there was only one thing that it needed. Something that would truly spice the place up and make it feel like home. *Color*.

They all laughed in relief. Paulina could not help but agree as she had told Celina to feel free to express herself as she saw fit and to make the guesthouse her own.

It was just a few hours before dinner and Paulina suggested they should leave their new guest to get settled in, because soon they should all start getting ready to go out to dinner.

"I hope you're hungry?" Paulina asked.

"I could eat a cow," Celina said jokingly.

"Great because you are in Cowtown, and that's just what we're having," Fernando replied. "I know a great steak house where we don't need reservations," he said to his wife with a wink.

In just a couple of hours, they all made their way back into the city for dinner. The sun was going down, and they each couldn't help but notice the Texas sky with rose-colored clouds overhead seemingly painted by the hands of God.

It didn't take long to get there, and Fernando found a parking spot right outside the front door. He thought how lucky he was to be with the two very beautiful creatures that he escorted into the restaurant. He took Paulina by the arm after opening the doors for them.

The women hadn't coordinated their outfits, but both wore short black dresses showing off their long, silky smooth legs. Paulina wore her shoulder-length hair up showing off her diamond ear studs, while Celina's long, curly hair reached to the middle of her back. Fernando also tried not to stare at the lovely décolletage each possessed.

"Party of three," he said to the hostess.

"Okay. It'll just be twenty minutes. Would you like to sit at the bar while you wait?" the young hostess said to them.

"Yes, that would be great," Fernando replied. "I don't know about ya'll, but I could use a drink," he said as he turned back to his companions.

Finding a small table by the window, Fernando pulled out the chair for Paulina, and Celina sat down and opened the beverage menu. Each decided to have a glass of wine; Fernando and Celina both had a merlot while Celina went with a zinfandel.

"I *love* your shoes," Celina said to Paulina. "I saw a pair just like that at Barney's in New York, but they were just too expensive," Celina frowned.

"Thank you! What size shoe do you wear? Maybe you can borrow them sometime?"

"Really? I'm a size six," Celina said as she leaned to take another look.

"Yeah, why not? In fact, you can look through my closet and raid it whenever you want."

The girls went on and on about designer clothes and shopping while Fernando sat there unengaged as he polished off his glass of wine. Finally, he interjected, "I should have got a Maker's and Coke."

"Oh, I'm sorry, dear, I forgot you were there. And what interesting topic would you like to talk about? Oh, let me guess, hunting? Oh, wait, how about how to change a flat tire?"

Celina not understanding the dynamics of their relationship just sat there in awkward silence, enjoying every minute of it. She always pictured him to be the dominant one in the relationship, but she was witnessing for herself who really wore the pants.

"Why do you always have to make me out to be the bad guy?" he said to Paulina with a smile. "I'm not the bad guy," he softly whispered to Celina.

"Oh, now I'm the bad guy? I don't have to make you out to be the bad guy, you do a pretty good job doing that yourself," she retorted.

He firmly took hold of Paulina's arm and looked at her straight in the eye and said, "You know what?"

"What?"

"I love you," he surrendered.

"That's what I thought," Paulina said confidently as she allowed him to kiss her on the cheek.

Relieved, Celina tried to stop shaking her legs because the next words she heard never sounded so great— "Fernando, party of three," the hostess called out.

They took their table, and they wasted no time ordering another drink while Fernando took the liberty to order some calamari for the table.

"Rude!" Paulina said. "There you go again. You didn't even ask if that's what we wanted," Paulina told Fernando.

"Well, isn't it?" Fernando replied

Paulina lowered her head and then looked up at him and said, "Yes. But you don't know if that's what Celina wanted."

"No, that's okay. I love calamari. That's one of the things you will like about me—I'll try anything once. If I don't like it, I'll tell you," she said innocently to Paulina.

"That's good to know," Paulina said.

It never took much for Paulina to feel tipsy. After two or three glasses of wine, she was usually done for the night. But for some reason, maybe as a confidence booster, Paulina seemed to be holding her own.

Fernando had always been the type of guy who could drink everyone else under the table, never once showing any signs of being drunk. Being more of a social drinker, Celina paced herself—not knowing what else was on the agenda. The next round of drinks came, served by a handsome young waiter evidently working his way through college.

As he took their order, Paulina noticed the way the young man looked at Celina. So Paulina winked at Celina, inclining her head to the waiter, suggesting that she make a pass at him. Celina picked up on Paulina's cue and began to flirt, telling him she was new in town and asking what he would recommend.

"Well, that would depend on your taste. Do you prefer chicken or beef?"

Celina replied coyly, "Neither. I'm into seafood."

"Well, to be honest, the seafood here isn't really that good. But, I know a better place. Why don't you give me your number, and I can take you there on my day off? That is, if your parents don't mind."

"No, we don't mind at all," Paulina replied kicking Fernando under the table. Fernando was not amused by his wife's flirtatious behavior, and suddenly began to feel a bit jealous for some reason. His face became pale and without expression.

His mind drifted off to a time when he thought Paulina had cheated on him with an old friend of hers from college. His insecurities nearly cost them their marriage, and they had to seek counseling for three months before finally he was able to overcome his fears.

Counseling worked beautifully at resolving his fears until he was forced to acknowledge that while his wife had always been true to him, they did have a serious marital problem. She yearned for more time with him.

Ever since the early years of their marriage, Fernando had been continuously out of town and didn't spend much time with his wife. Since their counseling sessions, he had made an effort to include her in his travel as much as possible, making sure that they had sufficient coverage at work so that things would continue to run smoothly without them.

When the waiter left the table, Paulina started asking Celina if she thought the young man was cute. But Fernando interrupted her, saying, "Alright, come on you guys, quit messing around."

Paulina apologized to her husband realizing she may have acted inappropriately. So she changed the subject to a question she had wanted to ask each of them from the beginning.

"Okay, let's get down to brass tacks. Let's talk about how all this is going to work. I've been doing a little thinking. I could put together a stronger marketing strategy for the gallery—especially when it comes to our website. I also want to use the Internet more effectively by asking customers for their e-mail addresses and by setting up a Facebook account for the gallery. That will allow us to showcase and sell Celina's work as she creates more pieces. We could also rent out some billboards all over the Dallas-Fort Worth Metroplex encouraging new business and stuff like that. About how many pieces do you have right now, Celina?" she inquired.

"Well, if you include everything from top to bottom, I would say around fifty or so. But of those, only around twenty are completed. I'm still working on the others, but they are mostly sketches and paintings. All but one of my sculptures is complete—that's the one you saw," as she turned to Fernando, "but the rest are all done and ready to be sold."

"Okay," Fernando engaged, if money weren't an object, what kind of supplies would you need or want to have?"

"Well, I pretty much have everything already," Celina said cautiously. "But I am going to need some new supplies soon."

Paulina countered "No, no. If we are going to do this, I want you to have everything you need. Now is not the time to be shy. Be specific. Like what?" she asked.

"Well, if money didn't matter, I would get a bunch of stuff."

Celina started naming off a few things that came to mind.

"Paint brushes, easels, and paint—but not the cheap stuff like I've been using—I mean real paint that professionals use. Spray paint, larger canvases, modeling clay, metal, iron, a welding machine, an industrial-sized oven— just to name a few."

"Now, we're talking," Paulina said with enthusiasm. "I hope you like to shop?" she said as she lifted her glass. "A toast to our new endeavor."

"Cheers!" they all said as they clinked their crystal glasses.

CHAPTER SEVEN

The Tour

That evening went just as they had planned. They finished their meal and headed home, still talking about how they could each contribute to their overall success. Once they were there, the women immediately took off their shoes each complaining of the rigors of wearing such high heels.

Fernando bid them goodnight, reminding Celina to set an early alarm because they wanted to show her around town. Paulina suggested that Celina stay in the main house until her things arrived. She showed Celina to a comfortable guestroom on the first floor with a queen size bed and a full bathroom of its own.

"Thank you so much for making me feel welcome," she told Paulina.

"Don't mention it. I'll see you in the morning."

The next morning, Fernando was up drinking coffee and reading his paper when he heard Celina greeting him.

"Good morning!"

"Good morning, Celina. How did you sleep?"

"Like a baby," she said as she yawned. I can't remember the last time I slept that well. Where are the cups?" she said as she looked around.

"Look in the cabinet on the left just above the counter."

Just then Paulina came down stairs and walked into the breakfast nook.

"Is that coffee I smell? I'm not used to him making me coffee," she said to Celina.

"Anita, our maid, usually makes it. I hope it's not too strong," she said poking at Fernando as she poured herself a cup.

"All right, is it me or do you guys enjoy picking at each other?" Celina curiously asked.

"Girl, wait until you've been married for ten years. You'll be doing the same thing. Trust me."

"Ten years? We've been that way ever since we were just dating," Fernando interjected.

"To be honest," he explained, "I love to argue. I think it's not only normal, but also healthy, in a relationship. It keeps us grounded," he said as he smiled at his lovely wife.

Paulina turned her attention to Celina. "Anyway, what do you want to see first? I thought maybe we could go to the zoo or maybe the museums. You know, Fort Worth has one of the best zoos in the Southwest and some of the best art museums in the country," she bragged to Celina.

Fernando had different plans in mind. He explained that there was only one way to take in the best of Cowtown, and that was to start at the Stockyards.

"Let the battle begin," Celina said to herself as she listened to them make their points.

It was like watching a tennis match between them when Celina finally interrupted, "Why don't we flip a coin?"

"No, he's probably right," Paulina reluctantly acquiesced.

"Besides, you're probably tired of seeing that museum stuff in New York City. I will admit the Stockyards are different and we haven't been there in a long time anyway. I hate it when you're right," she told Fernando as she hit him on the shoulder.

He could only grin; he didn't have to say a word, because the chagrined look on her face said it all. They set out to show off their city.

Fernando grew up in Fort Worth and knew it like the back of his hand. He considered himself more knowledgeable about the rich history of the city than any tour guide could ever be.

With its roots in the cattle industry, Fort Worth is said to be the spot *"Where the West begins."* Cowboys and rustlers once thrived in the town that was established as a military fort in the late 1800s. But Fort Worth is now one of the nation's fastest-growing cities with more than half a million people within its city limits. The Stockyards is one of the last reminders of how the town got its start.

Fernando had collected numerous books on Fort Worth, and as they made their way to the Stockyards, he began to tell Celina as much as he could on the subject. Celina could not wait to see it for herself.

"I wish I had a better camera," Celina commented ruefully as she pulled an obsolete model out her purse.

Paulina said, "You can borrow ours until we get you a better one. Did you remember to bring it, honey?"

"Yeah, it's in the case on the floor in the back seat. Take a look at it if you like," he said to Celina.

"Wow, it's nice," she said as she familiarized herself with it.

The first thing he wanted to show her was the renovated sheep and cattle pens that had been converted into restaurants and a retail shopping center known as The Stockyards Station. They went into the dozens of souvenir shops and tourist attractions such as the Livestock Exchange Building where cattlemen used to buy, sell, and trade their livestock.

They also visited the historic Cowtown Coliseum (built in 1901), which featured the best in indoor rodeo, as well as the Texas Rodeo Cowboy Hall of Fame with its collection of memorabilia dedicated to the preservation of the Texas Cowboy.

Throughout the streets were bronze inlaid markers that honored cowboys like Roy Rogers, Gene Autry, Bill Pickens and local conservators of the old West like Amon G. Carter Sr.

Celina was intrigued by what she was seeing, taking pictures of everything she could, while Fernando and Paulina stood back and were equally intrigued by her. Celina was truly in her element. She had a unique eye for seeing things most people normally miss. Adjusting the camera to different scenes, she changed lenses several times before asking Paulina and Fernando to pose for a few shots as well.

Celina asked Paulina if she had ever done any modeling, paying compliments to her tall, slim figure and the fact that her striking bone structure required little makeup to accent her natural beauty. Paulina blushed as she replied that she had always thought of modeling but never made the time to pursue it. Celina suggested she could do a simple photo shoot of her and explained how it could be done tastefully.

Paulina immediately agreed. She immediately began thinking what a great gift idea the photos would be for Fernando's approaching birthday.

In the midst of giving Celina the tour, Paulina thought about how much she loved the time that she and her husband was having—even if it was in the presence of another person. Paulina loved Fernando and longed to re-build their relationship as it was in the early years of their marriage. At times she felt inadequate as a woman because they had never had any children. Three miscarriages had caused so much grief and stress to their marriage that she and Fernando had ceased to discuss the possibility of a family.

On this day, she was noticing other happy families who had children, and Paulina commented out load to Fernando that they should try again.

Fernando, on the other hand, had got used to the freedom of doing whatever they wanted whenever they wanted. He actually also wanted to have children—but not at the risk of causing Paulina any more pain or the grief of losing another child. He consoled his wife as they continued to walk around with Celina. Celina was unaware of the reason why they didn't have any children; they saw no reason to tell her.

For lunch, they had the only option other than a steak when visiting the stockyards. Texas Barbeque.

At the restaurant, Paulina asked Celina what she thought about everything she had seen thus far. Celina said it was quite a treat to see all of the attractions and discover the history that surrounded them. The more Paulina found out about Celina, the more she enjoyed and felt comfortable with her. She could envision becoming even closer over time.

Paulina grew up as an only child and was not very close to other family members since most of whom lived in other states. As a child, Paulina played dolls by herself and even made up an imaginary friend just to have someone to talk to.

She never maintained any contact with her high school friends and quickly lost touch with her college friends. Celina was easy to talk to and despite her beauty, she was not arrogant or conceited. Both women had the qualities of humility and kindness in common.

During their late lunch, Paulina leaned over to Fernando and asked what he thought of going out later for a little dancing. She also suggested buying a nice outfit for Celina, as they were dressed for an evening out, but she wasn't. Fernando, of course, did not object to the idea of once again taking the two gorgeous ladies for a night out on the town.

The Tour

The first place that came to Fernando's mind was the world's largest honky-tonk. In addition to dancing and live music, it was a tourist attraction sporting an indoor rodeo, a huge arcade area, and dozens of pool tables.

Celina asked what they were talking about so secretively when Paulina asked her if she knew how to dance to country music. Celina had never been country dancing before, but that she wasn't entirely opposed to the idea.

Her only concern was that she realized she wasn't dressed to go out and asked if they planned on going home soon so she could change. Paulina told Celina of their plan to take her shopping.

Celina reluctantly declined saying that she didn't think she could afford to buy new clothes right then and there. Paulina told her not to worry about it and to consider it a gift. Paulina was not about to take no for an answer and insisted that Celina permit her to have the fun of doing this for her.

So the trio set out to do a little shopping for Celina and found the perfect shop on the corner of Main and Exchange Avenue. As they walked in, Fernando was immediately drawn to the bar they had inside.

Celina was shocked to see a bar in a retail store. It was not just an area where you could buy a beer, it was a full bar with actual horse saddles as bar stools.

"Only in Texas!" Celina said out loud. The girls paid no attention to Fernando as he sat and drank his favorite adult beverage (Maker's and Coke), while they did a little prospecting.

"I think this would look cute on you. Why don't you try it on?" Paulina said to Celina.

"Oh, that is cute! But what do you think about this one?" Celina asked loving every minute of it.

"That is nice. What size jean are you?" Paulina asked

"I'm about a six," Celina said as she took both to the fitting room—but not before grabbing just a few more things.

As she was trying on the clothes they had picked out, the thought crossed her mind that she was not used to anyone being so nice to her without any cruel or manipulative intention in mind. Paulina seemed genuine, and it was nice to know there were real and honest people out there who weren't looking to take advantage her for personal gain. She was used to people using her for her looks and not what she could offer as a person.

Paulina went to go check on her husband who was talking to a couple of people from out of town. She waited on him to finish, and then he asked her how things were going, and if she had sold the farm yet. She told him that Celina was trying on a couple different things and how nice Celina was, even though she didn't know her that well as a person. Fernando said that if she wanted to know something specific that she should just ask Celina.

That moment they saw Celina came out of the dressing room wearing a comical version of her idea of what a real cowgirl wears. She had on a huge cowboy hat (three sizes too big), a buckskin vest with extra long fringe, a long sleeved white dress shirt, and some extra small turquoise blue jeans accented by an enormous belt buckle in the shape of Texas that would make any wrestler proud.

"Want to help me pick out some boots?" she said arms extended and eyebrows lifted.

Paulina took one look at her, gasped, and quietly walked away as if she didn't know her; for once Fernando was left speechless.

An older woman wearing the same type of vest walked up to her and said, "That looks so good on you".

Celina thanked the woman, looked over at Fernando and pointing her finger accusingly said, "You still haven't said anything."

Fernando slowly cleared his throat and tried to think of a polite way of saying he was offended by how horrible she looked. Thankfully, Paulina arrived just then with a different outfit and accessories, saying, "That's good, but try this on instead."

A few moments later Celina came out wearing the outfit Paulina had picked out for her. Both Fernando and Paulina were equally stunned by how good she looked. Celina wore a light blue-colored long sleeved T-shirt, a black vest, and a pair of black jeans that showed off her figure.

Celina had every eye in the store upon her as she modeled them. Paulina immediately approached Celina and told her how good she looked and that she would have no problem finding a dance partner dressed like that.

Celina blushed as she accepted her compliment. Looking in the mirror, she saw that she could definitely get used to seeing herself dressed that way.

Fernando put down his drink and walked over to the girls. He noticed how Paulina and Celina were beginning to bond—laughing and joking around with each other.

Paulina asked him what he thought of Celina's new look, and he did not hold back from saying that he thought she looked very sexy. He was delighted that they could buy that outfit for her.

Although Celina was uncomfortable taking a gift like that, she really wanted the outfit and liked all the attention she was getting. They convinced her to wear it straight out of the store, but not before Celina insisted that they allow her to pay them back in some way.

Fernando told the store attendant to put the outfit on his credit card and went to the register to settle the bill.

Paulina told Celina she might have to take her up on paying her back. If she were serious about doing a photo shoot, Paulina had always wanted to do a portfolio for Fernando. Celina was excited to hear that and told her that as soon as she was settled in, they could start taking photos right away.

CHAPTER EIGHT

A Night to Remember

After a few more hours of shopping and showing Celina around, the three of them made their way to the dance hall. The sound of country music could be heard outside the main entrance, and, as they entered the club, a sea of cowboy hats crowded the place from end to end. Celina was thrilled to be there and started to sway back and forth with the rhythms, tapping her boots, and singing along.

They grabbed a small table near the dance floor that had a good view of the band. Reminding them not to miss him while he was gone, Fernando excused himself to go get some drinks. Celina took advantage of the opportunity to ask Paulina what she had in mind for the photo shoot.

Paulina explained that she wanted to take some pictures wearing sexy lingerie while posed in an elegant fashion for Fernando's birthday. Celina felt flattered that Paulina would allow her to participate in such an intimate gift and quickly agreed.

She told Paulina that it sounded like a lot of fun and that she couldn't wait to get started. Celina asked if she had already picked out something to wear—secretly hoping she would have another opportunity to go shopping with her.

Paulina said that she had a couple of outfits she could use but had something else in mind. A look of confusion overcame Celina as she tried to figure out what Paulina was saying. Paulina blushed as she explained that she wanted to do some of the photos in the nude. Celina's eyes widened in surprise, but as an artist she immediately began to envision Paulina in a naked pose.

Paulina began to feel aroused by the idea of taking pictures like that for her husband. The truth was that Paulina and Fernando had been losing their sexual attraction for one another, and she saw this as a way to bring them closer; after all, what man wouldn't like a gift like that.

Paulina loved her husband so much that she was willing to try anything to spice up their love life. They had done things like going to strip clubs together and picking up a few adult movies from time to time. They even brought toys into the bedroom and discussed different fantasies they had.

For the most part, they had avoided acting any of them out. She remembered one time during a drinking game that included a round of "Truth or Dare," she had asked Fernando what his biggest fantasy was.

To no surprise, his fantasy was to have a threesome with another woman. She told Fernando that she wouldn't be opposed to the idea and that she had often fantasized about that herself.

Back in college, she'd had an encounter with another woman whom she knew through a mutual friend. This woman had often flirted with her and told her how pretty she was. One night, after a party and a lot of drinking, she had indulged her curiosity with a night of passionate kissing and foreplay. They never took it any further.

Paulina told Fernando how good it felt to kiss and to be touched by another woman. The silkiness of her skin. The feel of caresses by someone so soft and passionate and yet forceful. She had often imagined what it would be like to be with another woman.

A few moments later Fernando came back with three schooners of beer and asked what he had missed. The girls just looked at each other and smiled as they told him they didn't even realize he was gone. Paying little attention to their comments he asked Paulina if she wanted to dance. Paulina wasted no time in taking him up on his offer and onto the dance floor they went.

Fernando was a great dancer, and Paulina enjoyed every minute of it. Holding her just above her waist and pressing his hand against hers, he twirled her around the dance floor as if they were the only two people out there. Celina looked in amazement at them thinking how lucky Paulina was to have a man like that. How she wished she could meet someone that she would have that kind of connection with. She began to think of her lost love, Jaime.

He was also a pretty good dancer and would sometimes take her to dance. She thought how awful it must be for him to be locked away in prison, and she wished he were there with her. She felt reluctant to tell her new friends about him, and that he was one of the biggest reasons that she wanted to move down there so badly. At least for now, she felt she must keep that a secret.

After a couple songs they came back to the table laughing and almost out of breath. Celina complimented their chemistry on the dance floor and vowed to one day be just as good out there as they were. Paulina hit Fernando on his shoulder and told him he had better take her to dance or he was not going to be getting any that night.

"Go on, dance with him," Paulina encouraged Celina.

"Oh, I couldn't," Celina shyly replied. "I can't dance that good anyway."

"Bullshit," Fernando said. "Come on just follow my lead. I promise not to step on your toes. Just don't step on mine," he said jokingly.

Fernando took Celina by the hand and led her to the dance floor amidst all the other people.

"Look, its simple. Take my hand and just follow my lead. Don't worry about anything else. Just feel the beat, and I'll do the rest."

He took her around the dance floor a couple of times, and Celina never broke eye contact with him. She could not help but smile the whole time, while the twinkling of the glass chandelier in the shape of a horse saddle sparkled on them.

The music took a change of pace switching to something a little slower then, and the two of them decided to head back to check on Paulina. Just before they went back however, Fernando turned to Celina and was about to ask her not to mention how they danced together back in New York.

But he came to his senses and decided that he didn't want to keep anything from his wife. He was simply going to let the chips fall where they may. Instead, he just asked her if she was having a good time. Celina replied ever so happily that she was, in fact, having a *really* good time and how happy she made the trip to Texas after all. They rejoined Paulina, and they swiftly grabbed their drinks—gulping down every last drop trying to catch up with Paulina who had taken the liberty of ordering another round.

Paulina complimented the way they looked together on the dance floor and said, if she didn't know any better, she would have guessed they had danced before.

Fernando interjected, "But that's true!" He told Paulina that the night before he came back, Andy wanted to go out to a nightclub and that was when he introduced Fernando to Celina. He went on to how she may not know how to dance country style, but she was a hell of a salsa dancer.

Paulina was feeling tipsy from all the drinks and winked at Celina saying she would have to be the judge of that the next time they went out dancing. She told Fernando that they would have to take Celina along the next time they went out for some Latin-style dancing.

The three new friends were having a good time laughing and joking around with one another. When the band took a quick break, the deejay started to play a mix of hip-hop music. Paulina and Celina hurried back to the dance floor hand-in-hand without asking if Fernando wanted to join them or not.

They held hands as they climbed on a small podium, then once in position, their bodies rubbed each other with every move. Celina had her back against Paulina's slender frame and Paulina rubbed her hands up and down Celina's long legs, thrusting her body slowly against hers.

Celina was also getting into the groove of the music and turned around to Paulina, grabbing her hips, and gently pressing her face to hers slowly while moving her lips down Paulina's neck.

Fernando was shocked and excited as he sat back and witnessed the women continue to dance. He thought how great it would be to have both of them dance that way for him one night.

Then just as he was about to get up and order a few shots of tequila to end their evening, he looked back at them to see the two of them heavily making out with each other. He watched in amazement as the two kissed and touched each other. He snuck his way to the podium and held them both while they continued to dance. Paulina placed her hand behind his head bringing him closer and began to kiss him and looked at Celina seductively as if to suggest this could be the start of something more intimate.

Fernando found himself in the middle of the two women facing Celina, and without thinking, he stretched out his arms to pull her closer. Paulina was turned on at the thought of the three of them possibly taking things a little further. She knew that any man would love to have his way with the two of them; Fernando was no exception.

Celina had always found Fernando attractive, and now she was finding them both appealing. Somewhere in the back of her mind, she was worried that this one night of tipsy passion could interfere with their plans.

But, the temptation of having them both was too strong for Celina, and they all allowed the night to take them wherever it might lead.

Fernando escorted them toward the door, letting them know that the club was no longer the appropriate venue for their lovemaking. They agreed knowing this was just the beginning of their adventure. They were eager to be in a more intimate setting where they didn't have to worry about anything except exploring their obvious lust for one another.

Fernando told the girls to wait for him by the door while he rushed to the get the car, which was just a few blocks away. The two of them staggered as they made their way towards the exit, laughing at each other and the way each was carrying on.

Paulina could barely walk straight, and Celina made fun of her, telling her how crazy she was for ordering that one last shot before they left the club. Paulina stated pointedly that she was never one to hold her liquor well and did not care to.

Fernando pulled up, and Celina helped Paulina into the back of the car. She held her close in the back seat, caressing her hair as Paulina rested her head on her shoulder. Paulina was feeling so light-headed that she couldn't see straight, but she could feel the soft warmth of Celina's body and the sweet fragrance of her scent.

An animal-like desire began to overcome her, and she reached out to caress Celina's breasts over her blouse. Fernando watched in the rear view mirror trying carefully not to wreck the car, as the women grew more and more intimate. Celina groaned in pleasure as Paulina's groping began to be more heated, and she slid her hands inside of Celina's blouse and under her bra to cup her breasts.

Paulina began to slide her tongue down the length of Celina's throat, and raised her blouse up to her neck. Celina arched her back so that the small, pink tips of her nipples were raised toward Paulina's eager mouth. Paulina brushed her lips over them gently, then swirled her tongue around the tips as Celina moaned in delight. Paulina pulled Celina's searching hands toward her own amply endowed chest and guided her left hand toward her throbbing vagina.

Celina felt the heat seeping through Paulina's silk panties under her skirt and began to massage her clitoris in a circular motion. Paulina grabbed Celina by the back of her hair and pulled her on top of her so that they she was lying on her back.

Fernando barely containing his erection, pressed his foot hard on the accelerator, and was trying to get home quickly before the girls had too much fun without him. He began to speculate on the possibility of these women developing feelings that were more than just sexual.

Within minutes, they were pulling through the gates of their home. Fernando drove straight to the garage and hurriedly opened the door for them. Paulina and Celina were breathless but began to laugh as they tried to untangle themselves from one another. Fernando grabbed Celina's waist from behind and pulled her out of the car, helping her steady her balance.

Her blouse was still raised up to her neck, and he could not help but to slide his hands up to her rounded breasts. He teased her nipples and pressed his erection against her buttocks as she grinded against him.

Paulina kicked off her shoes, took off her shirt and slid her skirt down to her ankles as she exited the car. She reached out to unzip Celina's jeans and slid them down along with her lace panties. Fernando yanked Celina's bra and top off, and pulled Paulina to Celina's front, so that Celina was in between the both of them. Celina writhed against them in a passionate embrace, as Fernando took off his clothes as well.

"Let's get wet," Paulina whispered as she ushered them toward the pool.

Celina smiled and said, "You already are," and Fernando chuckled at the both of them.

The girls gasped as they entered the cold water of the pool and shivered against one another. Fernando turned on the patio lights and quickly jumped into the pool, splashing Paulina and Celina. They screamed and splashed him with water as he swam toward the shallow end where they were squatting.

He picked up Paulina's legs and wrapped them around his waist and began to kiss her deeply. Celina watched yearningly, and eagerly joined when Fernando extended his arm to her and pulled her face to his wife's. Paulina and Celina kissed slowly at first, then more urgently as their desire grew. Their tongues swirled into each other's mouths as they tasted one another. Fernando pushed his straining erection inside of Paulina, while she was still kissing Celina and began to thrust his hips into her. Paulina moaned in pleasure as Celina lowered her tongue to her breasts and began to suck on them passionately. Fernando bucked against her wildly, and she screamed as she felt her first orgasm in months.

She unwrapped her legs from his waist and slid Celina back in front of her, so that Celina's back was toward Fernando. "Do you want him?" she asked Celina.

"Yes." Celina answered.

Fernando grabbed her by her neck and asked her again, "Do you want me?"

Paulina slid her hands in between Celina's thighs and began to rub her fingertips against her clitoris.

"YES," Celina moaned louder. Fernando grabbed her buttocks and spread them slightly open as he entered her from behind. Celina closed her eyes and held on to Paulina's shoulders and whimpered as he thrust inside of her. Paulina nibbled on her ears, neck and breasts. Celina and Fernando moaned as they both exploded in orgasm.

The three of them lay in the cool shallows of the pool equally out of breath and not having much to say to one another about what just happened. Paulina and Celina lay there still feeling the sporadic pulses that electrified their bodies.

Fernando was the first to get out of the pool, and he handed them towels to dry off. He asked them if they would like to go inside with him for a little while to relax before calling it a night. But Celina said she was tired and thought she should go to bed as she looked toward the guesthouse. Paulina told Fernando to go ahead without her and that she would be upstairs in a little while.

Sober now, and with only towels wrapped around them, the two headed towards the guesthouse to say goodnight. They stood outside the door and looked at each other.

Paulina told Celina that she thought that it might be a better idea if she continued to stay in the house with them, at least until her things arrived from New York. Paulina still felt the rush from having a night of the ultimate hot, steamy sex, and Celina could tell she didn't want it to end.

Celina felt the same way but didn't know if she should be the one to initiate it. Celina had never had a threesome before but had fantasized about having one once before.

A high-school friend who was dating a guy they knew in school used to come on to her each time they got drunk together. They would make sexual inferences from just about anything she said and would make suggestive overtures to try and seduce her.

She had been glad that she never went through with it. He was a loser who didn't treat her friend very well and eventually ended up cheating on her with another woman.

After that, she hardly talked to her friend anymore; the friend went pulled away after the incident, and eventually Celina lost contact with her.

She was left to think about what might have been—if the circumstances had been a little different. Celina saw Paulina and Fernando as a lot more secure and committed couple and was attracted to them both this time.

After a minute of thinking about whether or not she should stay inside the house, she agreed but asked Paulina if she minded if she smoked a cigarette before going inside.

Paulina didn't mind at all. She was going in to check on Fernando and would return to tell Celina goodnight. She walked inside to find Fernando getting ready for a shower. Paulina told him that she would be inside momentarily after she said goodnight to Celina. He told her to take her time and that he was heading to bed after he freshened up. Once in the shower, he began thinking to himself of the possibility of them creating an awkward atmosphere around Celina. He never intended for what had happened to happen, but it happened still. His relationship at that time with his new protégé was supposed to be strictly professional. "What did I do?" he asked himself.

A more unsettling thought entered his mind. What if Paulina and Celina became jealous of one another? Fernando knew that he was developing feelings for Celina that were deeper than physical attraction and lust. He recognized that Celina had several of the same qualities that he admired in Paulina. Both women were intelligent, passionate, and strong willed. Both women were dedicated to succeeding in their careers. If they became rivals for his attention, he didn't know who would win.

Beginning to sober up now, Paulina and Celina sat by the pool and talked about what an interesting night it had turned out to be. Celina finished her cigarette, while contemplating what she was feeling at this moment.

Neither one of them quite knew what to say to one other. Celina would begin to speak, then would stop herself and take another drag. Paulina knew what she wanted to say but didn't quite know how to get it across without making things even more uncomfortable.

Deciding it was too much for her to hold back, Paulina decided to just say what was on her mind and get it out in the open. "Look, I have something I want to tell you."

Paulina explained that she didn't want Celina to feel uncomfortable living with them after having shared such intimacy with her husband and with her. She especially didn't want for her to think that this would be an ongoing thing—part of their living arrangements. Paulina was raised to believe that same sex relations were wrong, and she didn't want to mislead Celina about that.

Celina listened to everything Paulina said carefully, giving her full attention as she shivered and wrapped her towel tighter around her cold, goose-bumped skin.

"I never thought I could share him with another woman before. I feared he might like it too much, would want her for himself one day, and leave me. But with you, somehow it's different. I have all the right reasons to be jealous of you, yet I'm not. It's as if things are just the way they were meant to be. I'm not sure how to explain it."

When Paulina was finished, Celina took her turn. She chattered nervously, "I'm grateful you said what you said. What just happened here was not my intention at all."

Paulina's eyes began to swell with tears as she smoothed her hands over her arms to keep herself warm. "If anyone should be jealous here, it should be me. I mean, I look at you and him together and everything that you guys have, and I think to myself, what a lucky couple. What you guys have together, most women would die for. All my life I have always seemed to attract the wrong type of man. The good ones never stay, and the bad ones never seem to go away," she laughed as she tried to make light of the situation.

Celina swallowed the lump in her throat as she explained her last thought. "I would understand if you don't want me to stay. But please, before you ask me to leave, let me just say this." She bowed her head in remorse for her behavior. Her breathing became heavier before she looked up at Paulina and said, "I would never come in between you and Fernando.

I know I just met you, but I can almost see us all like family. As for me and you behaving the way we did, I really didn't care for it too much." She quickly tried to retract what she said stumbling over her words.

"I...what I meant to say is, you were great, but I'm just not into girls." Her bottom lips pouted as her eyebrows rose. "I hope you understand, it was something that just happened in the moment."

Suddenly, it wasn't as cold outside anymore. The wind seemed to stop blowing as the moonlight blanketed them all the warmth they needed. Paulina scooted closer to her and took her hand in hers.

Paulina leaned toward Celina saying, "You have nothing to worry about. I don't want you to go. It would be my pleasure to have you stay here with us." They rested their heads on each other as they sat there looking up at the stars before heading in.

CHAPTER NINE

Settling In

A few days passed and a new workweek was about to begin. Fernando and Paulina decided to stay at home with Celina to wait for her things to arrive from New York. Paulina advised Fernando that she could use that time to straighten their financial records for the gallery, and if he didn't mind helping Celina alone. Knowing she had a better grasp that that sort of thing, he agreed and went outside to tell Celina.

Once the movers got there, he began to help Celina set up her belongings. Celina was excited to finally have all her things with her. It was beginning to feel like home for her.

As Celina unpacked, she began to sort through the items she wanted to keep and things she didn't need any more. She came across memorabilia that reminded her of her mother, her childhood, her friends and even things from past relationships that didn't work out. She opened a box labeled "private" and began to sort through its contents. She pulled out an old t-shirt she hadn't worn in a while that reminded her of her boyfriend Jaime.

One day after coming home from a local bar, they had gotten into yet another argument. Only this time, he accused her of looking at another guy suggestively and before she knew it, he had hit her hard across her mouth.

She kept this bloodstained shirt over the years as a reminder never to be mistreated again. She asked Fernando for a hanger and tucked it away in a closet along with of all of her other things, never mentioning the incident or Jaime.

Fernando was amazed at some of the things she had made, especially the smaller pieces that she created out of clay and bronze. He began to separate artwork from personal belongings, thinking those pieces could easily be taken to the studio for quick sale.

"We are going to have a lot of fun working together once we get you all settled in," Fernando said. "I can't wait to see how well we are going to do considering how talented and creative you are."

Celina was flattered and took that as an opportunity to ask him when he thought would be a good time to start shopping for some of the materials and supplies she needed to begin working on other projects. Fernando didn't hesitate to tell her that, once they finished unpacking, they would go inside and get online to research where to buy some of the materials right away.

Excitement and gratitude lit Celina's face. She asked if she could make dinner for them since their maid Anita had the night off.

Fernando's eyes lit up because he never realized she liked to cook too. He began to wonder what other hidden talents she may have up her sleeve. "So you like to cook? He said as his stomach began to growl.

"I have always loved cooking, but I seldom get the chance since I am always so busy in my studio," she said with a slight frown on her face. "Do you think Paulina would mind if I cooked for you?

"Not at all," he exclaimed. "In fact, I think she would be very pleased if you did. Paulina loves trying new things. She is a lot like me in that way. We try to eat at different places whenever we can. What did you have in mind? He wondered as his taste buds were tingling in his mouth.

"I can make you some traditional Brazilian food that my mother used to make for me when I was just a little girl."

"Mmm! Now that sounds like a plan," Fernando said.

They spent the next few hours talking to one another like they had never done before. They told each other almost everything. From how and where they grew up, places they have been, and things they would like to do in the next few years. They discovered that they had more in common with one another than they realized. It was more than just a love for art that they shared in common.

Of course Fernando, being much older than Celina, impressed her even more because of his life experiences. He shared with her how difficult it was on him growing up trying to fill the role of a father figure to his siblings after their father died. He looked at her sincerely, telling her that he knew what it was like to lose a parent. It was never easy for him to talk about his father's death to anyone. But he felt that telling that story to her seemed natural, as if telling it to someone he had known all of his life.

Then he mentioned how growing up in his neighborhood was not an easy task either. Because of the friends he had growing up, he almost joined a gang. He was glad that he didn't, because most of them either ended up in prison, on drugs or dead. But he said like her, some of his teachers took a liking to him and made themselves available to him whenever he needed. They saw something in him that was different. He wasn't all about trying to be a tough guy like most of the boys he grew up with. Instead, they saw him as a young man who, with the right guidance and direction, could make something of himself.

Celina listened to him attentively. As they sat on the floor directly in front of each other, they both reached out to pick up the last box that needed to be unpacked. They nearly bumped their heads as they scooted closer. They waited a moment before pulling back and found themselves staring into each other's eyes. In that moment, they forgot their surroundings and what it was they were supposed to be doing. She leaned in closer to him slowly and her eyes grew heavy. He tilted his head and slightly opened his mouth, fighting back from pressing his lips to hers.

He quickly pulled away and gently said, "Listen to me telling you all of my sad stories. I didn't mean to make you so sad." To which she replied, "You didn't make me sad. Not at all. Thank you for telling me." Then he told her that they better start making their way back to the house so that they can begin shopping and getting ready for dinner.

Once they were finished unpacking and decorating Celina's apartment, they made their way into the main house and into the kitchen. Fernando asked for Paulina's help to look for art supplies and hardware stores—but mainly it was because he knew that she had a better sense of their budget and didn't want to overspend.

Celina wasted no time searching the cupboards and raiding the refrigerator for dinner supplies of her own. Celina discovered in disbelief that there was hardly any food available. At first she thought, "What do these people eat? How could these rich people not have any food to eat?"

Then she realized they must eat out a lot, or that Anita must buy a little at a time because they were hardly ever home.

Seeing the troubled look on her face, Paulina asked her what was wrong.

Celina turned and said, "Why don't we order pizza instead? Then I can help you guys look for what we need."

Grinning, Paulina looked at Celina and agreed knowing what she must have found looking for food in the pantry.

Fernando replied, "Well, if that's the case why don't you guys look for all that stuff while I start thinking about who I can invite to Celina's debut party at the gallery. What do you want on your pizza?" he asked as he pulled out his cell phone.

The three of them sat around the kitchen table, eating pizza, and checking out various web sites for art supplies. Even though Fernando was looking forward to having this whole thing come together, he couldn't help but to keep an ever-watchful eye on how much expense everything was adding up to.

Paulina didn't so much as to bat an eye on the cost of the supplies they picked out, but once they tallied up the final cost Celina began to think of what she could do without. Celina was not used to being pampered like this and started to feel a little pressured that she would have to produce so much work so soon. She was used to working at her own pace—usually because of budget constraints.

Just then Paulina stood up to put away her plate and said "That wasn't too bad. I thought we were going to spend way more than that." A sigh of relief broke from Celina and Fernando as they got up from the table and headed to the living room.

Fernando began making a list of people he could personally invite to Celina's grand debut and came up with a list of over 200 guests. But it would also be a public affair. Anyone would be able to attend for a nominal admission fee.

So he began to create an event on the new De La Mar Studio Facebook page so that over the 3,000 friends listed there could also attend. The event was to happen in two months time, and it would consume him all his energy and enthusiasm to throw such a gala affair at his gallery.

He envisioned the event: the gallery would be packed full of people with huge searchlights outside the entrance casting over the city at night.

Christie would greet people as they walked in and hand out small brochures while the twins Eric and Alex would tend the bar; the staff would all be dressed formally.

The three of them tossed around different ideas and shared a few laughs about just how giddy Fernando seemed to be about everything. After talking about their plans, and how busy they were going to be for the next few weeks, they called it a night so that they could get an early start the next day.

Morning came on Celina's first day to begin actually working for them. This was also the first time she would be formally introduced to the other workers they had at the studio. You could sense the nervousness from Celina as they approached the gallery and began to enter the studio from the back entrance. She didn't know what to think or what to expect. But as nervous as she was, she was equally as enthusiastic and couldn't wait to get started.

Trying to contain her emotions, Celina confidently followed them into the back of the gallery. As usual, the twins were in the warehouse. One was wrapping up some paintings, and the other was sweeping the floors. The mild sound of traditional Mexican music echoed in the background as one of them sang along with the tunes. They both looked up at them as they walked in and saw that the De La Mar's had a new face joining them today.

They began to stare simultaneously and unintentionally at the young, beautiful woman they had with them. Fernando casually turned down the radio to introduce Celina to the twins.

Paulina in a firm voice said, "Come on, guys. How many times do I have to tell you not to leave a mess on the floor? You know I don't like to see it like this."

Alex replied, "I know, Mrs. Paulina. I was cleaning it up right now. Please, let me get this out of your way."

Fernando saw the frustration on his wife's face and interjected by saying "Hey, guys that can wait. I want to introduce someone who's going to be working with us. Eric, Alex, this is Celina. Celina these are the twins that work for us." The twins examined their new friend, exchanging handshakes and making little effort to hide what they really thought of her by the admiring looks on their faces.

Celina kept her poise despite picking up on their subtle gestures. Paulina didn't have any real reason not to like the twins because, after all, they were good workers and would do anything they were told. She just didn't like how sloppy they had become over the past few months. She saw people much like the way she saw art, for what it could be as opposed to what it was.

Fernando asked Paulina to take Celina inside and introduce her to Christina. As the girls began making their way into the gallery, the twins slightly turned their heads and followed Celina with their eyes.

"Okay, guys listen up," Fernando said. "Let's set a few ground rules here. Celina is going to be working here at the shop sometimes, so I really want you guys on your best behavior. Meaning, I don't want you guys disturbing her while she's working. If she needs anything, she will ask you for it. More importantly, we're planning to have an exhibition of her art work in a couple of months, and Paulina is probably going to be harder on you until all this is over. Having said that, I want both of you to be prepared to tend bar that night. I'll let you know in a couple of days exactly when it's going to be, and I'm counting on you two to be there."

"Okay, whatever you say boss. But let me ask you one thing. Do we have to wear a tie?" Eric asked.

"No, you don't have to wear a tie. But I'll most likely have you guys dressed all in black or something like that. I don't know, we can figure all that out later. For now, just keep doing what you're doing, and I'm sure everything will turn out just fine. Deal?"

"Yes, of course. No problem. Sounds like fun," they said.

Fernando met up with the girls in the show room to find them engaged in deep conversation about several of the pieces on display. Paulina's face showed how impressed she was with Celina's knowledge of the different styles and the origins of each artist whose work was on display.

He was puzzled by how well they were getting along with one another. For some reason, he expected his wife to be more reserved and less friendly—as she was with their other workers. But they seemed to be connecting with one another, completely independently of his influence.

Furthermore, Fernando could not deny his attraction to Celina. He felt that in a profound way, Celina completed a part of a puzzle that he and his wife lacked. She fit in their lives perfectly. She was innocent, creative, self-motivated and open-minded. He began to think if had he never met his wife, Celina would be the kind of person he would consider having a relationship with.

Fernando felt a pang of guilt as Paulina momentarily broke eye contact with Celina to smile at him. He knew he loved his wife very much but still could not help but think of what it would be like to share his life with Celina as well. Watching the two women interact brought another startling thought to him.

What if Paulina could allow him to engage in a romantic relationship with Celina? The word polygamy popped into his mind, and he began to wonder what it really meant. Out of curiosity, he decided in his spare time to begin searching the Internet for all he could learn about it.

He knew that if Paulina found out what he was up to, she would not be too pleased. He could probably get away with it if he didn't tell her right away. In their entire marriage, he had never kept any secrets from his wife, but he had an unexplainable desire to find out more on the subject of polygamy and to pick up all he could learn like a magnet to a tray of nails. He made a note to himself in his phone to remind him to start his research later.

He went out into the showroom to find out what everyone else was up to. Paulina told him how impressed she was with Celina's knowledge of all the work they had on display. Although she wasn't familiar with any of the artists, she could relate to them individually by way of some of the things she had made herself. She understood the use of color on the paintings, the canvas and the tools the artists had chosen, the way those choices could make the art come more to life. She knew the way to use the right kind of light in the photos, and how the speed of the camera could make things appear more than life like. She had explained the process of how to make a masterpiece with clay.

Celina soon captured the respect of the entire gallery with her explanation of how to put it all together—leaving everyone speechless in admiration. Celina seemed to blossom like a butterfly coming out of its cocoon in the eyes of all the workers, not to mention Fernando and Paulina. Celina had a way of making complicated things seem so simple by explaining in a way that anyone could understand.

"Oh look at me," she said humbly. "I didn't mean to go off like that. I just get so passionate talking about art so much, and I tend to forget how boring I can be."

Paulina shook her head and said "No! Quite the opposite, I assure you. It's not every day I get to hear it come from the artist themselves talking about all of the hard work and effort it takes to create such things."

Christina agreed, telling her that she was never aware of how complex the things she took for granted everyday were. She told her that she would never be able to see anything in the gallery the same way again after her explanations.

Fernando's phone began to ring from an unknown number. It was the delivery people calling to tell him they were on the way to the gallery with Celina's artwork. Soon a huge semi pulled out in front of the gallery. Fernando instructed the twins to take each item to the back as they brought them inside the front door as quick as possible so they didn't interrupt traffic any longer than was necessary.

The first things to be unloaded were boxes of clay and bronze sculptures, busts and statues covered in bubble wrap. Celina's heart raced faster and faster in excitement as she watched them carefully place each box on the floor. The next things that came out were paintings, murals, photographs and etchings.

Paulina and Christy stood impressed with all they saw as they both snuck peeks at everything that flowed through the door. The last thing to exit the truck was an enormous crate that had the sculpture with which Celina had originally impressed Fernando.

Fernando insisted that one was to stay outside to be the first and last things people would see who came to the gallery, just as he envisioned.

For the next few hours, everyone helped put everything away and consulted on re-arranging the showroom to display their latest artwork. All the crates were carefully inspected, and every piece checked to ensure there was no damage. The women were in their element as they strategically decided where each piece should rest.

Fernando once again admired how well they complimented one another telling them if he didn't know any better, he would think they were sisters. They smiled at him thinking how silly he was for being so playful, but they appreciated him for being such a visionary and for his love of his work and his family.

The time they would spend together over the next few weeks would prove to be more than enough for them to get to know each other on many levels. They each began to bond more and more as they shared stories of their childhoods, their love for the arts, and how much they each respected the gift of life, love and family values.

Even after ten years of marriage, Fernando and Paulina showed sides to one another that neither one of them ever knew about. They found it funny how Celina allowed them to bring out certain innocence to their relationship. They felt more than comfortable discussing all matters in Celina's presence, as if she, for some reason, brought them closer together. It was as if Celina was a missing piece to a puzzle long forgotten. Now they looked forward to waking up and going to work and discovering what each day had in store for them.

Since Fernando was home more often, his love life grew more passionate with Paulina as well. She had become used to him being gone so much, and she hadn't realized how much she enjoyed having him home. Having him around also allowed him to become more involved with their finances, relieving some of Paulina's demanding tasks, too.

Celina began to appreciate how well Paulina ran their business as well as her household. Her own mother was independent by necessity, not having a partner to depend on. Celina admired Paulina's independence as well as her loyalty to Fernando. Paulina began to teach Celina about stocks and investments, and how to spend and save wisely. She also taught her how to negotiate better prices from wholesalers, despite having several contacts already that offered them ridiculous prices because of Paulina's parents' position in the community.

Celina began to feel like she was part of a real family and that she truly mattered to the two people she had shared her heart with.

All of her former insecurities seemed to disappear, and this change was becoming apparent in her artwork. She used bolder, brighter colors in her painting and tried different lenses for her camera shots. Fernando's praise of her new work was also extremely encouraging.

Fernando was very proud how Celina was blossoming into a mature and confident artist. He enjoyed watching her create, and sometimes destroy, different pieces without asking anyone else's opinion of them. He felt that he and Paulina nurtured Celina's creativity while also giving it direction. The three of them had never felt happier or more satisfied with life than when they were together.

CHAPTER TEN

Discovery

Over time, Fernando found himself continuing to research polygamy. He had been raised to believe that traditional relationships were based on a two-partner team. However, being raised by a single parent allowed him to view marriage objectively.

His mother had said she loved his biological father immensely, but also loved other men that came into her life after his father had left. Although she had never married more than one man, she had been able to love several different men within a short time frame.

Fernando did not see his mother as being an adulteress or even a bad spouse or mother. She had followed her heart. He began to wonder if it was possible for someone to love another person in addition to whom they are married, and still be devoted to each other.

One day, while Paulina and Celina were busy inside the gallery he stepped into his office to get on his computer. He logged on to a discussion forum about polygamy that he found fascinating, but he hadn't had the courage to comment on. He wanted to be open-minded about the whole thing and as unbiased as he possibly could. The particular discussion of the day was regarding why it was illegal in America for a person to have more than one spouse. He realized that thousands of normal people all over the United States were in successful polyandrous marriages and were just as happy as anyone in monogamous relationships.

He found out the differences between polygamy, polygyny, polyandry and plural marriage. He read multiple blogs and toured many websites and found all he could on the subject and every time he did, he was left to ponder the same question; why was it wrong? Neither Fernando nor Paulina knew of anyone who had that kind of relationship and knew very little about it. The only thing he ever knew up until that point was that it was wrong in the public eye, against his religion and that it was illegal. He focused his research on those three things.

He discovered that the first reason why people were so against it was largely because of the "popular" religions' negative depictions or lack of information about it. He realized that people usually tend to go along with whatever they think is normal to begin with, especially when it pertained to plural marriage. He thought of the saying, "The bigger the lie, the more people will believe it," and how it became normal to believe it was wrong over time.

Never once in all the times he had been to church did he ever hear a sermon on what the bible said about polygyny. Yet in several places in the Bible people like Abraham, Jacob and even King Solomon who was said to be one of the wisest men that ever lived, practiced it. He couldn't find any passages in the Bible that said it was wrong.

But Fernando did not want his view on plural marriage to come strictly from a religious standpoint. As a Catholic, he was led to believe it was wrong, not because he was directly or specifically taught it was, but rather simply because it was considered left wing by the church's standards.

One of the biggest misconceptions he found was that society believed polygyny was invented by a particular church or religion. But he learned that it was simply a way of life that was practiced since biblical times that became unpopular as the power of the Roman Catholic Church grew. But it became evident to him that those that had several wives in the bible had them for practical reasons.

That night, as he and Paulina were getting ready for bed, he brought his laptop with him so that he could study. He had made himself some hot chocolate and slipped into his favorite pajamas while she was putting her favorite lotion on her hands and feet. She asked him if he was working late on something and if she could help, thinking he was doing something for their business. He told her that he wasn't working on anything, but that he was doing research on something he had been studying for a few weeks.

He had been eager to tell her all he had found and of the new feelings he began to have, but he was afraid of what she might say or how she would react for spending so much time on it. Then before he knew it she glanced to see what he was looking at on the computer. He was reading a blog on polygyny. The caption read "The Advantages of Polygyny."

When she asked him what he was reading, he tried to mask his look of surprise and guilt, as he was not fully prepared to begin discussing this topic with her. He told her how involved he had been in conducting his research on it and began to probe her on what her thoughts were on the subject. When she began to tell him what she knew about it, to his surprise she wasn't as unfamiliar with it as he had suspected. Like most people, everything she had ever heard about it was negative.

She had heard about people from up north who dressed funny, and who lived on compounds where the women were forced to marry older men against their will. She knew of those few perverts in cults who would marry underage girls. She also had heard that boys were exiled from their homes when they came to the age of puberty. The boys were forced to live on the streets because they became a threat to the older men when it came time for them to take a younger bride.

She also thought that mainly people from Utah practiced it because of religious beliefs they were taught which said that by practicing polygamy they would receive riches in the kingdom of heaven.

He laughed as he agreed with her because that was pretty much all he had ever known, too. He crawled into bed with her and began to share with her all that he had begun to know. They discussed how people were so adamant against other people who chose to live together in plural marriages, and how most people believed it was wrong. He explained that primarily because of taxation purposes, it was illegal in America. Since the United States enforced a separation of church and state, no religious entity could determine how many wives or husbands a person could have.

However, despite having the right to contract as set forth in the Bill of Rights, the IRS could charge a person for fraud if they filed more than one tax return. They read how the civil judicial system would rather avoid how to determine who would get what in the event of a divorce. The more they read and the more they talked about it, the more they found themselves talking in favor of having that kind of relationship. They agreed that if people loved each other enough and could set aside any jealousies, there shouldn't be any reason why they couldn't share the love they had for one another with someone else.

After a couple hours of talking about it, he asked his wife what she thought Celina would say if they were to ask her to be a life partner with them in a plural relationship. But before she answered, she turned to him and asked if he were serious.

He put down his now cold cup of hot chocolate, sat up and leaned to her and said, "What if I am?"

"Well I don't know. What do you think she would say? I don't want her to think we're some weird couple you read about or see on TV or something."

He laughed and said, "I think she would be more concerned about what you would say. After all, I am your husband and this is not something that most people are used to."

They deliberated the repercussions they would face if they decided to pursue a plural relationship. They knew that almost no one would understand that it could be a healthy addition to their existing household to have another person join them in a long, lasting committed partnership like that.

"I tell you what," Fernando suggested, "Let's sleep on it. And if you still feel the same way in the morning, why don't we ask her and find out what she thinks?"

It took them three days to work up the courage to ask Celina if she wanted to be with them in a committed relationship with them. They had fun debating how they should bring it up to her. Should they both do it? Should just Paulina? Should Fernando do it by himself? Finally they agreed to bite the bullet and do it together. They decided to discuss it with her after dinner and no matter what the outcome, they would not go back on their decision to pursue a plural relationship, be it with Celina or someone else down the road.

Paulina asked Anita to make a special dinner for them she conjured up by herself. It was to be a three-course dinner. The appetizers were to be three kinds of cheeses, on three types of toasted bread crackers. Three cheese chicken penne Florentine was the main course with three large white chocolate dipped strawberries apiece for desert.

"So how did you like your meal," Paulina asked coyly.

"Oh, it was great. I'm stuffed," Celina said as she pushed her cup of strawberries away from her.

"I haven't eaten like that in months," she joked.

Celina noticed how subtly strange the two of them were acting when she added, "If I didn't know any better, I would think you two were up to something."

"It's funny you should say that," Fernando said looking across the table at Paulina who was smiling nervously trying to keep her leg from shaking. Paulina looked at Fernando expectantly when Fernando turned to Celina and said, "Okay, Celina we want to ask you something very important, and I hope you don't feel awkward after I tell you what we have to say."

Celina squinted her eyebrows and tilted her head in confusion before saying, "Um, well, too late. What's going on?"

Paulina took a deep breath to settle her nerves when she anxiously said to Celina, "Okay, I'm just going to spit it out. You know that we both care about you a lot right? And I think you can see for yourself just how much Fernando and I love each other by now."

"Yeah, so... Just tell me Paulina. I'm sure it's not that big a deal," she said as she patted Paulina on her trembling leg.

"We've fallen in love with you."

Celina's eyes widened as she just heard another woman tell her that she was in love with her. Not to mention that so was her husband. Celina was speechless for moment as she tried to absorb Paulina's speech.

"Having you here with us these few months has opened our eyes and our hearts to a lot of different things. I can't explain it. Fernando and I care about you so much. We only want what's best for you."

Paulina told Celina what they have been talking about and why they have been acting so funny the last few days. Celina looked dazed as she envisioned in her mind everything she was being told and tried to take in everything like a dry sponge that was placed in a pool of water.

In short, we were wondering what you would think about being a part of our lives for good."

"Like what do you mean?" Celina asked bewildered.

"Have you ever heard of a plural relationship or plural marriage before?" Fernando interjected. They spent the next hour explaining all they knew of those kinds of relationships to her and answered all the questions she had on the subject as well as any misconceptions she may have had. Sharing Fernando with Paulina would not be her first choice of the kind of relationship she would prefer. Mostly because she didn't know how Paulina would feel, knowing her husband would be intimate with her alone on some occasions.

Paulina assured her that she would do her best not to feel that way, and that they would be better off taking things slowly in the beginning. She also thought it best to redefine the relationship they had for one another.

Paulina advised Celina they would no longer be intimate with one another like they had been in the past. She apologized if she made Celina uncomfortable for having a sexual relationship with her and assured her that was not her intention.

They all agreed that in order to make their relationship stronger, they would not engage in sexual threesomes from that point forward. They also thought it best for Fernando to spend the next few nights with Celina alone, in a kind of a courtship. By doing so, it would also give Celina a way to understand what to expect from the couple, especially from Paulina who was to share her husband.

"I have to be honest with you," Celina started to say. "When I first met Fernando, I didn't know he was married. I thought he was handsome, charming, and a very respectful man. Of course, I also knew he was successful and I admired him for all of that. When I learned he was married, I was surprised. It didn't even occur to me that he already had someone special in his life. Then when I met you, I thought, what a lucky woman. I was kind of jealous of you at first."

"I thought, why couldn't I ever be that lucky to meet a man like that? But now that I've lived with the both of you, and seen you two interact, I realize that you are both lucky to have found each other. But, you most of all, Fernando. Paulina is truly one woman in a million, and I can't even begin to express how blessed you are for having a wife like her."

The women exchanged their gratitude for one another, which bonded their friendship even further. For the most part, the night was going the way they had planned. They spoke about the proposal respectfully, intelligently and rationally. They weighed all the pros and cons just to be sure, but the matter of jealousy kept surfacing.

Fernando took it upon himself to help diffuse the issue from outweighing the other matters at hand when he said, "I think that it would be common for a woman to have those tendencies based on how they are treated by the man." The women looked at him in full attention.

"In other words, if the man spends more time with one of the women, of course she has a right to become jealous. If the man favors one of the women more than the other in any obvious way or gives more attention or special treatment to one over the other, it would naturally cause jealousy. But if he made an effort, he could spend about the same amount of time with each of them, providing love and attention to each, as fairly and equally as he could, then it would lessen the chance of the women becoming jealous."

Paulina turned to look at Celina and said, "For now, we just want you to think about everything carefully before deciding what you want to do. No matter what you decide, I don't want you to feel uncomfortable about any of this. I just hope you know that you can talk to either one of us about it whenever you have any questions."

She also told her that if she didn't enter a relationship with them, they would most likely pursue finding someone with whom they could partner.

Celina asked Paulina why she felt so strongly about doing this, and if it was okay if she did a little more research on it before giving them her answer.

Fernando gave her the names of websites, blogs, and a few communities he knew online that could help answer any questions she may have. They left Celina to think about what they told her, and both kissed her goodnight before going to bed.

Celina sat in stunned silence on her bed, enjoying the stillness around her. She was afraid that if Fernando and Paulina had spent another five minutes talking about polygamy or plural marriage, she was going to run screaming from the room. What kind of person did they take her for? Celina wrapped her arms tightly around herself and tried to make sense of their entire conversation.

A husband and wife had just professed their love for her, just a few weeks after relocating her into their backyard! A more pressing question was what kind of people were *they*? The thought of them luring her into their lives for reasons other than her artistic talent alarmed her.

What if she wasn't talented at all? Was that why she never made it in New York? Did she make a mistake in leaving too soon? Were they some kind of sexual, predatory couple? She began to feel panicked by all of the thoughts swirling in her head. She pulled her knees up to her chest and pressed her forehead against them, trying to avoid hyperventilating. She inhaled slowly through her nostrils and exhaled deeply from her mouth.

"Calm down," she chided herself, "you're making this way too hard on yourself."

Just then, a gentle rapping at the door made her jump, startled.

"May I come in?" Paulina's soft voice called from the other side.

"Yes," Celina said, unwrapping herself from her ball of comfort.

Paulina smiled as she walked in carrying a colorful Mexican quilt. "I forgot to give this to you earlier," she said as she unfolded it on the end of the bed, "I saw it in a magazine and thought you would appreciate it."

Celina watched Paulina's expression carefully, as if seeing her for the first time. Her face appeared mothering and loving as she looked over her surprise gift to Celina. There was a small smile on her lips as if the gift were a secret for just the two of them.

As Paulina described what type of fabric it was made of and by what artisan, Celina listened intently to the gentle tone and inflection she put on each word. The Texan twang combined with the unmistakable Mexican accent was soothing and familiar to Celina. She watched as Paulina slid her hand over wrinkles, smoothing them out, and thought how graceful her movements always were.

This beautiful woman is in love with me, Celina thought to herself, suddenly feeling a rush of pride mixed with the warmth of happiness.

She placed her hand over Paulina's and said, "I love the embroidery, it's beautiful!"

"I thought it matched your pillowcases that you love so much," Paulina smiled and clasped Celina's hand in hers. "I wish I could've met your mother. She must've been a remarkable woman to have raised someone as gifted as you."

Celina felt tears begin to prick at her eyes. Paulina immediately swooped down to hug her.

"Oh I'm sorry! I didn't mean to upset you," she said as she kissed the top of Celina's head.

"No, it's okay. It's not you. And I'm not sad," Celina assured her as she hugged Paulina firmly, "I'm happy. I'm so happy and so lucky to have met you and Fernando. And I do love you both very much."

Paulina smoothed down Celina's hair gently in the same manner as she did the blanket. "I believe we all found each other for a reason, and I'm not going to waste one minute worrying about what the world will think of me and the people I love," Paulina cupped Celina's face in her hands and pecked her on the cheek.

"You get some rest now. I'm sure you have a lot to think about."

Celina yawned and stretched out across the bed in agreement.

"I do need rest," Celina said with her eyes closed, "But for once, there's nothing to think about. My head and my heart are in complete agreement right now."

CHAPTER ELEVEN

Celina Meets the Parents

Over a month had past and the three of them had spent a lot of time together really getting to know one another. Their love for each other continued to develop more and more. Fernando and Paulina had already made most of the plans for the art show, and they deliberated about inviting Paulina's mother and father to the affair since they lived so far away.

Paulina's father, Jesus Rivera, and her mother Petra came from wealthy families in Mexico but lived just outside of Austin in the Texas hill country on a vineyard. Mr. Rivera made his wealth by way of oil and gas interests, communications and technology and sat on the board of several companies in Austin.

He was very involved in Texas politics, and his circle of friends included senators and congressmen, lawyers and doctors. He was considered one of Austin's elite as a prominent businessman. In his spare time he enjoyed playing golf and tending to the horses they owned, while Mrs. Rivera spent most of her time caring for the vineyard and devoting her energy to charities.

All and all they were living the American dream and loved their only child Paulina very much. When Paulina told her parents she was going to marry Fernando they were not entirely thrilled to say the least. They asked her why she was choosing a man who was so beneath her. They did not like that he did not come from a good family and that she could do so much better. The night she told them she was engaged, her father was so upset he even threatened to remove her from his will and never speak to her again.

Mr. Rivera told her that she was throwing her life away by marrying this man and that Fernando would never be able to support her and provide for her they way *he* envisioned for her. He wanted her to marry someone rich and successful like one of his friends--a surgeon or a lawyer or someone in politics. But instead, she wanted to marry this random older guy she met at an art show in Dallas that they both sponsored. In the beginning her mother, Petra, shared Jesus' resistance for their daughter getting married, but over time grew to love and accept Fernando as a part of the family.

Fernando was the eldest of three children. It was Fernando, his brother Joseph, who everyone called Joe, and his sister Rosalinda, who everyone called Rosa.

His parents were the children of farmers and crop pickers from Mexico. His father, Gerardo, was a tile setter with rugged hands from working with tile and grouts most of his life. He walked funny because of years of working on his knees. He was not an educated man, spoke very little English and did not want his children to suffer and struggle as he had. He spent very little time with the kids because when he wasn't on a job site somewhere, he was too tired to be as involved with them as he would have liked to be.

He died in his late twenties just before Fernando's eighth birthday. He had managed to save some money by putting it away without his wife knowing. He met someone who conned him into giving it all to him to invest in a business deal that later he found out was for drugs. It turned out to be a deal that had gone wrong, and he never saw any of that money ever again. The pressure and stress this loss caused him was too much for him to bear, and eventually he became a drunk and later committed suicide.

It wasn't until Fernando and the kids were teenagers that they found out how their father really died. At a family reunion, they overheard a family member talking about it with their mother. Fernando waited to confront her until later that night when he tearfully asked her for the truth. Until then, he thought his father died of a heart attack. After hearing the details his mother reluctantly provided him, he vowed never to be like his father or allow someone to influence him so much.

Fernando grew to resent his father for what he had done, but in some ways, knowing the truth about his father's death made him a much stronger and better person. He took his father's weakness and turned it into attributes that would account for Fernando's stubbornness and his lack of trust in people.

Celina Meets the Parents

Despite their reservations, they agreed to call Paulina's parents to tell them of the art show they were having so that they could have the chance to introduce Celina to them. Paulina called her mother and told her what they were planning. Her mother invited all of them to spend a weekend at their place in Austin.

Paulina was excited at the idea of going over there, but Fernando did not share her enthusiasm. He reminded her that he didn't appreciate being around her dad, who did not try to hide the fact he didn't care about Fernando very much. She told him it would make her happy to be around her family, and she really wanted to take Celina down there to see where she grew up.

On the way to work one morning, Paulina turned around to tell Celina that she had some exciting news to share with her. Celina's eyes lit up as she sat forward like a child buckled in the back seat of the Rover but wondering what Paulina had to say.

When she told her that she wanted her to meet her parents and spend the weekend in Austin, Celina said how great it would be to get away for a little while, and how she would be honored to meet the Rivera's. But she also expressed her nervousness about meeting them and asked what kind of people they were.

Paulina described them as a normal couple that lived alone and had been married for more than thirty-five years. Fernando's eyes rolled as he listened to Paulina downplay his in-laws to Celina and chose not to say anything. He just hoped that everything would go well as he had planned by taking her.

Celina asked when they were thinking of going to visit Austin wondering if she had enough time to prepare. Fernando told her that they were leaving for the coming weekend—one week before Celina's big show.

As they pulled up to the gallery, the women were about to go straight to work as they routinely did every morning, but Fernando wanted to call a quick meeting with all the staff before they started their day. He asked Celina and Paulina to wait in his office while he gathered the other three. Thankfully, the twins bought doughnuts that morning and Christy had a fresh pot of coffee made.

Everyone met in Fernando's office wondering what was going on. As Fernando took his seat in his high back Italian leather chair, Eric asked him if everyone was getting a raise or should they just start packing up.

Everyone smiled and shook their head at him but said nothing as Fernando took a deep breath and spoke.

"I wanted all of you here because, as you all know, our big art show is in two weeks. I wanted to include everyone in exactly where we are with the planning, and what we still have yet to do."

Christy and the twins let out a sigh of relief and listened to everything else he had to say. Fernando had taken the liberty to jot down a list of things that were already taken care of and a few small things that needed to be addressed before the show.

"Okay, so far all of the invitations have been sent out and of the 200 on the guest list, 178 have confirmed they will be attending. A few museum and art gallery curators will attend; a few critics I know from local newspapers and magazines are going to review the show. There will be some collectors, dealers and other influential art communitarians as well.

Keep in mind, this is an open door event, and I expect to have around another 500 to 700 people stop by over the two- day period. This means everyone has to be at the top of his or her game. Expect the unexpected, as I always say."

Everyone stayed quiet while Fernando was speaking, and Celina couldn't help the smile that fixed itself upon her face.

"Okay, guys, I'll need you to go and pick up the champagne on Tuesday so make sure you schedule that in-between your deliveries.

"Now I know you guys don't want to wear a suit or anything, so if you could just wear a nice black button-down dress shirt with black pants that would be great."

"Oh, and babe, if you could remind Anita to take a couple of my suits to the cleaners, I would appreciate it."

"Christie if you could also wear a black dress that would be great as well."

"I was thinking of setting up two bars—one on each side of the room. The guests that have a wristband will be those that I have personally invited, and those people also drink for free so keeps your eyes peeled. Those that don't have a wrist band will pay two dollars a drink."

"There will also be a podium at the front for you, Christie, to check in the guests. Remember, those with invitations will get in for free and everyone else pays twenty bucks admission."

"That reminds me," he said as he tossed Eric his keys. "There is a box in the back of my car that has some flyers I had printed. Can you hang some up on the windows for me? There is also a big billboard that you can put by the door reminding people of the event and that also advises that half the proceeds will go to charity."

"Okay, does anyone have any questions?"

"Can we bring some of our friends, Mr. Del La Mar? Christie said as she batted her eyes at him.

"Sure, I don't have a problem with that. But you're responsible for them. I don't want anyone underage drinking," he said as he gave a stern look to the twins.

"Okay, well, if no one has any more questions..." then he remembered one more item.

"And oh, one last thing, we are going out of town this weekend so we will not be in on Friday. So if you need anything, he paused, you know my number. Okay, let's get to work."

The week passed by with very few problems. Each night during the week Fernando drove the van back and forth, carefully taking some of Celina's artwork to the studio. Everything was going as he had planned.

Thursday came around and they all began to pack for their trip. They had planned to leave first thing in the morning, but everyone stayed up all night packing and telling stories from their childhood. They were having a good time and laughing at how three people from such different backgrounds all came to be together.

Suddenly Fernando looked at his watch and it was one o'clock in the morning. He quickly gave the girls each a kiss on the lips, wished them a goodnight, and headed upstairs.

Paulina stayed a few extra minutes with Celina to tell her goodnight and to say how happy she was to introduce her to her parents. Celina asked her if she planned on telling them about the three of them and what they might say when they found out. Paulina told her that she didn't think they would take it very well, but that she wasn't ashamed for anything they were doing. Paulina was happy that she was in their lives, and Celina shouldn't be ashamed either.

When Paulina said goodnight and went to bed, Celina went over in her head what she had planned while they were down there. She planned to ask

Fernando for the car for a few hours to visit some relatives that lived nearby. She was going to tell them that she had an aunt and some cousins that she wanted to spend a day with.

But in reality, she was going to go to the prison in Bartlet, Texas, just north of Austin where her ex boyfriend Jaime was. She had already made all of the arrangements by sending him letters and telling him that she was living in Texas now and how much easier it would be for her to see him.

In the beginning, she had told him how much she loved him, and how she missed him. But that was before she got romantically involved with Paulina and Fernando. It seemed as though she was in a robotic mode when it came to Jaime. Acting one way in front of the De La Mars, then remaining in a fantasy world about her ex.

She dreamed that he was the one for her and that she would one day give him children and become a housewife for him. The reality was, he didn't care about her. He only cared about himself, and he would use her for money, a roof over his head, and whenever he wanted sex. He was very selfish about spending money on himself instead of what should have been for them. He would constantly buy lavish gifts for himself, his friends, and family—but never for her.

But she didn't see him as a bad man for doing things like that. She thought that he was just a man who didn't have too much growing up and deserved to treat himself every now and again. He was always out and about doing his own thing, coming home every other day, and on the days he would come home, he would come in drunk and smelling of cigarettes and beer.

He never saw her creative genius and on many occasions would try to encourage her to quit making art. He would tell her that he was the man of the house, and if anyone were going to provide for them it would be him. Mostly he wanted her to quit working because he was fearful and insecure that she would meet someone else and would run off with him.

Knowing all of that, she still convinced herself that she loved him. But the truth was, she didn't have that many relationships growing up and simply clung to him because he gave her attention that she had longed for all her life.

What was funny, was that her friends saw right through him and all of his ways and would tell her to dump him. But she would tell her friends, "You don't know him like I do. You don't see him for who he really is deep down inside. Besides, I'm the one who provokes him to make him angry."

At that time, she wasn't doing so well as an artist and the money from her sales would not have sustained her in the apartment alone. In those moments, she thought she was kind of stuck with him and tried to make the best of it. Over time it just became a way of life for her, and she got used to working less and less and growing more dependent on him.

Pretty soon, he was in full control of her life—never allowing her to have many friends—and those she did have would have to come to their house to see her. He would tell her not to wear certain things and would get upset when she would attempt to wear makeup and fix her hair. He told her that a woman as beautiful as her didn't need to do those things to be pretty. The fact was his fear of losing her was the real reason, and he saw these comments as a way of making her feel good and at the same time holding her down.

A few more hours passed, and they were on the road. They took the back roads most of the way before jumping on the interstate. It allowed them the time to talk more about everything that was going on. The show, meeting Paulina's family, what they were like, and where their lives were heading together were all the topics of conversation.

A few more hours and a few pit stops later, the scenery changed to rolling hills nestled with wildflowers and honeybees. The only things that accompanied them in the landscape were American paint horses and Texas longhorns. The smell of fresh air and baled hay was so rich that city life seemed to disappear. Soon they found themselves on a blacktop two-lane highway with grapevines as far as their eyes could see.

"This is it," Paulina said. "This is where I grew up."

Celina was speechless as the house in the distance grew closer and closer. As they slowly pulled into the drive, Fernando extended his hand to enter the code at the gate and alert his in-laws they were finally there.

The house was unlike anything Celina ever seen before. It was an old house that was built at the turn of the century and that the Rivera's had renovated into the beautiful hacienda they called home.

On each side of the road that led up to the house were freshwater ponds and long fishing piers that stretched out into the middle of the water. Willow trees rested behind several benches strategically positioned around the water. The ponds each had irrigated pumps in the middle that gave them the warmest welcome so that even the novice fisherman couldn't resist.

But to Paulina, it was just an old house that she had spent lonely summers in. To Fernando on the other hand, it was really a place that he didn't care about being in either, but he was looking forward to spending some time out by the pond and maybe doing a little horseback riding. As they parked and began to gather their things, Paulina's mother Petra came out to greet them.

"Welcome! Please, leave all that there. We have plenty of time for all that. Let's go inside and sit down. I'm sure you all are tired of being on the road."

Paulina gave her mother a peck on her soft, lightly wrinkled cheeks and said, "Oh it's so good to see you. I've missed you momma."

"I missed you too, Paulina. You are getting prettier and prettier every time I see you."

"Hello Petra, Como estas?" (How are you?) Fernando said as he gave her a small hug. "You're looking good," he said to her as he held her hands in his.

"Gracias, gracias," she replied as she laid her eyes on Celina who was standing by the car.

"And you must be Celina," she said to her.

"Yes momma, this is Celina. The woman I was telling you about," Paulina told her mom.

"It's so nice to meet you, Mrs. Rivera. I've heard so much about you."

"Please, call me Petra. Well, come on inside. Your father's waiting to see you."

Petra escorted Celina into her home while Fernando and Paulina followed. They entered the house to find Paulina's father coming down the stairs to bid them welcome. He had just waked from a nap and still had the signs of sleep in his eyes. But his eyes glistened and his dark wrinkled face lit up at the sight of his only child, Paulina.

"Daddy!" Paulina said as she stretched out her arms to hug him. "How are you? I haven't seen you in forever it seems."

He kissed her on the cheeks and returned her hug, but looked past her shoulder at Fernando and replied, "It has been a while," as if to say it was because of Fernando that she hadn't come around that often.

"Hello, Jesus, it's good to see you," he said to his father-in-law and reached out to shake his hand.

"Jesus, I'd like to meet our friend, Celina," he said to him as he gestured toward Celina.

"Hello Mr. Rivera, it's a pleasure to meet you," she said timidly as she reached out to take his hand. "Thank you so much for inviting me into your home. It's really beautiful."

Everyone settled in their prodigious living room and began to make small talk about their drive down there and what the weather was like in Fort Worth. Fernando excused himself and asked if anyone else would like a beer before he headed to the kitchen. Jesus paid him no attention keeping his focus more on connecting with his daughter.

Celina was the only one who asked if he could bring her back a beer by softly saying "I'll have one."

"So, Celina, Paulina tells me you're from New York," Petra curiously asked her. "This must be quite an adventure for you to come to Texas all alone. Do you have any family nearby?"

Celina saw that as a fortuitous break to present her plan to visit Jaime. So she answered Mrs. Rivera by telling her that she had an aunt and two cousins who lived in Austin and that she yearned to see them. Fernando coming back with drinks in hand asked her why she never said anything to them about them before. Celina replied with a sad look on her face how everyone just seemed too wrapped up with all the planning for the show and that she didn't have the chance.

She also told them how a few weeks ago she called her relatives to tell them she would be heading that way soon, and how she would love the chance to visit with them. She explained, however, that she didn't have a car and that she wouldn't be able to do that even though she would be just a few miles away.

Petra interjected that they should loan her the car so that she could visit her family. Paulina agreed by telling Fernando what a great idea that was while Celina began to smile from ear to ear agreeing how great it would be. Fernando nodded his head and told Celina he didn't mind that at all, and it would be good for her to go and visit her family for a spell.

Jesus abruptly changed the subject, and looked at Paulina saying how he wished the next time they visited he hoped they brought grandkids.

Petra exclaimed, "Aye, Jesus! Don't start!"

Jesus replied, "Well, I'm just saying. I'd like some grand kids. They could at least think about adopting if he can't give her children."

Fernando just smiled as he was used to taking those kinds of stabs and said, "We're still having fun trying to make one. Why don't you guys consider adopting grandkids in the meanwhile?"

Paulina sighed in exasperation and told her father and Fernando to stop. She asked them, "How was your trip to Puerto Vallarta?"

"We actually went to Imanta, Punta Mita, Mexico, instead. They just opened a new resort, and we wanted to try it out before the gringos did," Petra said snidely.

"Gerardo asked about you," Jesus said to Paulina suggestively, ignoring the scowl on Fernando's face.

"Really?" Paulina asked sarcastically, "And have his table manners improved? He's chewed with his mouth open since we were thirteen."

Fernando coughed to hide a chuckle as Jesus once again changed the subject and turned his attention towards Celina.

"So are you a serious artist or do you do this for vanity?" Jesus asked without expression.

Celina balked and said wide-eyed "I've never thought much of myself to do anything out of vanity. My art is based on what I see in others."

"She's an excellent artist," Paulina said defensively.

"Of course she is." Petra said patronizingly, clearly trying to stay agreeable.

"And how old are you?" Jesus said bluntly, never breaking his gaze from Celina. "You look young enough to be his daughter," again stabbing at Fernando.

"Twenty-five," she answered

"Do you have children?" he asked.

Fernando and Paulina looked at Celina expectantly.

"No. I don't have any children. I'd like to—someday. But, no. No children." Feeling as if she were on an interview, she paused.

"Well, that's good. You're still young," Petra said. "You still have plenty of time for that later on."

Now Fernando, wanting a change in subject, asked how their wine business was doing and stated that it would be nice to take back a few cases to serve at the show. Although he didn't care too much for Jesus, he respected him as a businessman and was aware of the influences he had in the political arena.

Jesus now engaged Fernando's interest and began to speak to Fernando civilly since the discussion had now turned to him and his vineyard.

A couple of hours passed, and one of their servants had already taken their bags to the rooms they were to stay in. Paulina suggested they go and get ready and wash off the road dust since lunch was around the corner. Paulina and Petra gave Celina a quick tour of the house and left the men to themselves to size up each other's penis.

Celina was fascinated with the interior of the house and with some of the artwork they had collected from around the world. While Petra was trying to explain the history of a painting they had, Celina's thoughts were plotting a way to escape their traps and ask for the keys to the car to go see Jaime.

At the first pause in the conversation, she made up the story that if she were to go and see her relatives, that she should leave right then and get that out of the way so as not to disturb any more of their weekend. The women agreed and told her that she should just slip out, and that they would tell the men where she was so that they didn't worry.

Celina's dastardly plan began to unfold and off she went.

She took the short drive to go and see Jaime who had been expecting her all day. When she arrived, it wasn't long before the guards called her name and brought him out into the visiting room. She anxiously waited along with dozens of other people, and then she saw him enter the room dressed in an orange jumpsuit and house shoes. They were separated by bulletproof glass and were carefully being watched by overhead cameras and security guards. He sat down and immediately asked what took her so long to go and visit him.

She explained how difficult it was to leave her hosts to come see him, but that the important thing was that she was there. She was so happy to see him. He told her how miserable it had been for him not having his freedom, and how he was not eating well. He told her that she didn't have any reasons now not to see him more often and should make more efforts to see him now that she was closer.

Celina agreed with him, telling him that now that she was living in Texas she promised to do exactly that and not to worry about her devotion to him. She promised she would do better. She explained that she would also start sending him money so that he could go to the commissary and buy some of the things he needed to make his incarceration more comfortable.

He told her that he had been thinking of a plan for when he got out, and that she should tell the De La Mar's that she wanted him to move in with her in their guest house for a little while as he was an old friend of hers. He asked if she could make it so the De la Mar's didn't feel awkward about him staying there a short while.

As he was telling her his plans, Celina began to feel guilty for even thinking about doing such a thing to Paulina and Fernando because she had already began to feel emotionally attached to them.

She thought to herself that they didn't deserve to be betrayed by her because of how much they had done for her and how much they cared about her. Her face became semi-blank as he was talking so much, and he asked her what was wrong. She regained her composure, changed her demeanor, and shrugged it off by telling him that she was just trying to fight back her excitement about finally being together again.

After another hour of talking with him, one of the guards tapped her on the shoulder and told her that their time was up. They both stood up and said their goodbyes. Celina watched him as they escorted him back to his jail cell.

She left the prison and got back into the car to drive back to town. On her way there, she began to break down in tears because the visit that she had planned for over two months had not gone as she expected. Inside she was torn between the life that she thought she wanted, and a life she wasn't 100 percent sure about.

She wrestled with the idea of why she had gone to see him in the first place, and how it would have been so much easier just to let him go when she had the chance. She started to realize that she didn't care for him the way she had thought she did, and finally she began to see him the way everyone else did.

He was just using her to get what he needed and only had his own self interest in mind. She remembered how little effort he ever made to make their relationship work. To him, she was just a toy. He just played with her emotions and fed off of her free spirit.

When she pulled back in to the Rivera's house, she took a quick look in the mirror to touch up her makeup and to make sure the swelling in her eyes had gone down. She didn't notice, but Fernando was out on the pond trying to catch some fish and saw her pull up. He wondered what could be taking her so long to get out of the car, so he put down his fishing rod and began to walk towards her.

She saw that he was walking up the drive and took a deep breath before getting out of the car. She smiled at him and asked if he had any luck. She told him how much she loved fresh fish. He said the fish weren't biting that day, and it must be the old outdated lures Jesus had given him to use.

"So how did it go?" he asked. "How did you like seeing your family?"

"It was okay," she explained. "Things are just so much different now. I guess that's what happens when you lose touch with people. You tend to see them for who they really are and not who you thought they were."

Fernando didn't know what to make of her as he tried to understand what she meant. He started to ask if she was okay, but before he could she gave him a short hug and told him that she appreciated him for letting her use the car. Before letting him go she softly whispered in his ear that she loved him and gave him a small kiss on the cheek.

Fernando still puzzled, told her that he loved her too, and that he was glad to see her back. Recognizing that something had gone wrong, he told her not to let whatever had happened to her bother her. He told her that he and Paulina were her family now, and he didn't like to see her so sad.

"I hope you don't mind Fernando, but I just want to put that visit behind me for now. I just want to get back to doing normal things again—with you guys. Where is Paulina?"

"She should be inside getting ready for dinner. Why don't you go inside and get ready? Paulina should be upstairs. I'm sure she would like to see you. Go on. I'm just going to put back all this stuff in the barn. I'll be up soon."

He walked back to get all his gear together feeling confused and wondering what could have happened to Celina in those few short hours. He thought she would be in better spirits having seen her aunt and all her cousins. But he knew that when the time was right, she would tell him. Or, if she didn't, she would tell his wife. He knew that Paulina wasn't very good at keeping anything from him anyway. So either way he would soon find out and would be better prepared to talk about it then.

CHAPTER TWELVE

A Truth Unfolds

Everyone dressed formally for dinner at Jesus' insistence. The Rivera's had an old Chippendale dining table that they had bought from Sotheby's many years ago and only used for entertaining. Jesus even made it a point to tell everyone where each would sit as if they were children. He placed Celina on his right and Paulina to his left with Fernando next to Celina and his wife across from him.

Tall white candles accented the small wood-burning fireplace and the smell of seasoned oak permeated the room. It reminded Paulina of when she was a child and how they hosted important guests. Two uniformed servants served herbed rib roast with mushroom gravy, mashed potatoes and black peppered green beans. The wine was a special blend of his own private collection.

"Jesus, I have to admit you really know how to eat down here," Fernando declared as he lifted his glass.

"I would like to make a toast." All lifted their glasses.

"To family," Fernando proclaimed. The clang from the crystal caused chills to ripple down Celina's spine because she had never been a part of a real family before. But there she was with the people who had taken her in and treated her better than anyone else ever had.

"So tell me Celina, what kind of artist are you?" Jesus asked.

"I consider myself to be a conceptual artist and sculptor. I bring to life many different things I envision. Just whatever inspires me really," she trailed off lamely.

"And what inspires you, Celina?" Petra cross-examined.

"Well... life," she answered slowly, picking at her napkin. She could feel sweat beginning to prick at her palms. She pictured herself in a dark room with a spotlight on her face, like someone being interrogated in a cheesy crime film.

"Celina is very talented, daddy," Paulina said encouragingly. "That's why you need to come to Fort Worth next weekend and see for yourselves. You are coming aren't you?" turning to her mother for support.

"We wouldn't miss it for the world," Petra replied reassuringly, smiling as Jesus scowled. "So tell us more about the show. Have you invited a lot of people?"

Celina, relieved by Petra's gentle tone, described like a schoolgirl how Fernando took care of all the details and made all of the arrangements. As Celina spoke about the event, she began to soften Jesus' stonewall disposition and he appeared to be genuinely interested in her excited chatter.

Fernando and Paulina watched as Celina's innocent charm swept up the older couple. Jesus had finally stopped scowling and Petra was smiling warmly at her, as if she were a precocious child at show and tell.

"Did you enjoy your visit with your family today, Celina? I bet they were happy to see you," Petra said as she changed the subject.

Celina stumbled on her reply. "Umm... It was okay," she said, not meeting Petra's gaze. "Things don't always go the way you picture they would. Since my mother passed away, I haven't been a part of a real family," she said sadly, feeling the pain of the words as she spoke them.

"My father left us when I was very small. I can hardly remember anything about him, and I don't know any of his relatives. I get the feeling they don't care much about knowing anything about me either."

Fernando took Celina's hand in his without hesitation and Paulina simultaneously said firmly, "Well, you have us now."

Jesus watched them carefully, noting the intimacy the three of them appeared to be sharing. Petra thought their gesture was sweet and agreed with the couple telling Celina any friend of theirs was now a friend to her, and that she should consider their home her own.

Feeling Jesus' suspicious gaze on them, Fernando asked him for a nightcap over a game of pool in the game room. "Sure. What is it now? Seven games to five, right?" Jesus bragged.

"Yeah well, I hate to beat a man in his own house," Fernando countered.

"And you're in luck," he added. "I brought you a real Cuban cigar, so you can give your brand a rest."

Giving the women a chance to bond more, they went to Jesus' expansive game room where only a select handful of people had ever played pool on his twenty-five thousand dollar table shipped from England.

As the evening wore on, everyone's spirits seemed lifted, until it was finally time to retire to their bedrooms. Paulina kissed her parents goodnight and thanked them for being so hospitable to everyone. Seven bedrooms sat adjacent to one another down a long hallway on the second floor. Paulina and Fernando slept in the room across from the Rivera's with Celina's room diagonal to theirs.

Paulina excused herself from their room to bid Celina goodnight.

"I wish you could stay with us," she said as they embraced.

"Me too," Celina said longingly.

After a few moments, Paulina softly said "Okay sweetie, I better go before my parents see us. I'll see you in the morning, love. Fernando will be by shortly to tell you goodnight."

"Okay Paulina," she said in a low voice not wanting Paulina to leave her alone. Paulina returned to her room and asked Fernando to wish Celina a proper good night before going to sleep. Fernando quietly walked across the hall trying carefully not to make any sound and quietly tapped on her door. She gently opened the door trying to keep it from squeaking.

Still feeling down because of the memory of her mother, Celina began to tell Fernando how grateful she was that he had chosen her to be with them, but he kissed her on her open mouth before she could finish. He leaned in to her pulling her closer to him and kissed her passionately. Suddenly, they were interrupted by a blast of light as Jesus flipped on the light in the hallway.

"What the hell do you think you're doing?" he screamed. "How dare you disrespect me in my own home!" he said to them furiously. The roar of Jesus voice was that of a lion. The sound of his rage pierced through the walls like a knife through butter. Paulina, who was lying in bed sat up in disbelief wondering what could have happened.

As if they had synchronized their timing, Paulina and Petra opened their doors to witness Jesus chastising Fernando and Celina for what they had done. They quickly released each other's grasps and took a stepped away from each other, as if to imply Jesus had the wrong impression.

"Look, it's not what you think," Fernando tried to deflect Jesus' outrage.

"I saw the whole thing, you lying son of a bitch! I stood there watching the both of you, just as you started to kiss her," he said accusingly, pointing his finger at Fernando.

"And you" he turned to Celina, "What kind of a woman does this to her friend's husband? You must be nothing more than a whore Fernando found while he was out of town! Did you think you could fool me with your innocent little girl act?"

"Dad, wait a minute. You don't understand" Paulina said desperately. "You see…"

"NO!" Jesus interrupted her, "You don't understand! Do you know what I just caught your husband and his little tramp friend doing? DO YOU?"

Petra stared in disbelief, hoping it was all a bad dream while pulling the drawstring to her robe tighter and attempting to make sense of everything. "What happened? What's this all about?" she asked distraught.

"I just caught these two making out!" he exclaimed furiously.

Paulina and Fernando looked at each other wide-eyed and Celina stood behind them with her head down and her hands covering her mouth to stifle her sobs. She looked at Paulina and whispered, "Oh my God, I'm sorry."

Paulina slowly shook her head at both of them knowing that she was going to have to tell her parents the truth, even though she was hardly prepared for it.

"I want you out of my house this instant!" Jesus stepped aside and motioned for them to leave.

"Jesus please, just listen," Fernando pleaded.

"I said get out!" he yelled, reaching for Paulina, "Come here, mija. I told you he wasn't good enough for you. I told you he would only bring you pain," he said consolingly.

With her eyes closed she put her hands on her head and said almost shamefully "Dad, wait. There's something we need to tell you."

"Don't tell me you knew about this!" he demanded angrily.

"Can we just please all go to the living room? Please?" Paulina begged her father as tears streamed down her face.

Jesus cursed as he relented and ushered everyone into the living room asking himself aloud if his guns were loaded.

A Truth Unfolds

The two of them sat on either side of Celina across from Jesus and Petra who was now crying not knowing what to make of all that had happened.

As Jesus handed his wife some tissue to wipe her eyes, he said in a slow and deep voice "What can you tell me that would make this any better, Paulina?"

Her hands began to sweat and her knees started to shake as she tried to find the courage to tell her parents about their relationship with Celina.

"Look, Jesus," Fernando attempted to explain.

"I don't want to hear a word you have to say! As far as I'm concerned, you are not my son-in-law! You are nothing more than a..."

"Let them speak, Jesus" Petra said exhausted. "Let them speak."

All the attention funneled to Paulina like a black hole in the outskirts of space. She gathered her composure as best she could while she tried to think of the best words to use to her father. She finally said, "We are in love. We are all in love... with each other."

Jesus sat back on the couch in disbelief as he listened to her describe the dynamic of their relationship. Paulina began to tear up at the looks of disgust and shock on her parents' faces.

Celina turned to Paulina and put her hand on her shoulder said remorsefully, "This is all my fault. I didn't mean for any of this to happen."

But Paulina shook her head firmly. She took Celina's hand then Fernando's and proclaimed, "We have nothing to be ashamed of."

"Paulina! What do you mean you have nothing to be ashamed of? You're living in sin! We raised you better than that! What has he done to you?" Jesus glared at Fernando menacingly.

He turned back to Paulina and said, "I will not allow you to live like this. If it is your choice to continue on with this man and this...woman," he spat the word at Celina, "then I will have no choice but to disown you. I did not raise my only child to be a lesbian or a harlot. And your mother will agree with my decision, so don't ask for her forgiveness or acceptance or sympathy. You both have everything because of me and without me, you will have nothing!"

"Dad, I am not ashamed for anything we are doing. In fact I love this life we have chosen. I don't expect you or mom to understand. We don't expect anyone to understand. But if you love me, you will learn to accept this and move on. We are the same people you welcomed in your home just a few hours ago. Fernando loves me; I love him. And we both love Celina."

Her tone began to change from misery to anger, "And saying that what we are doing is a sin is like saying that fishermen are murderers. It only depends on your perception of what is right or wrong. You go hunting, dad, right? But I wouldn't call you a murderer or a killer. Even though the Bible is clear when it says "Thou shall not kill." It doesn't distinguish what you can't kill does it?"

She paused while she allowed her words to sit in with her parents before admitting the entire truth. "Dad, Mom… we want to live together in plural marriage. We plan on asking Celina to marry us. That is, if she'll still have us."

Celina's eyes filled with tears as she inhaled deeply. She didn't realize they wanted to *marry* her. Tears began to cascade down her face like a brook into a stream.

"Jesus, I realize you have never really cared for me. You have always made that very clear. I know you expected your daughter to marry someone rich and successful like you. But I have loved your daughter since the day I met her. I have been good to her, and we have done well over the years. Wanting to marry Celina doesn't change any of that. We believe that it will only enhance our love for one another. Since we met her, she has brought nothing but joy into our lives," Fernando said calmly.

He stood up and walked behind the couch where Paulina and Celina were sitting and humbly said "You say that we are living in sin. Well, before any of this came to be, I used to think the same way you did. How could any man be in love with his wife and fall in love with someone else? It didn't make any sense. It goes against the grain of everything I was ever led to believe.

Then I began to research what plural marriage was. What I found was the truth. And the truth is, there is nothing wrong with it. Not even from a biblical point of view. But our belief in this doesn't come from any religious teachings."

"But the church says it's wrong because the Bible says it's wrong, so it must be a sin" Petra said after blowing her nose.

"I thought the same thing but where does it say it's wrong? I couldn't find one verse or passage where God said not to have more than one wife. In fact, any time the Bible mentions men having more than one wife, there is no indication that it wasn't a normal, healthy family structure. It was never encouraged, of course, but it was portrayed as being part of an everyday normal life in those times."

"Yes, Fernando, in those times," Jesus said.

"Right. But ask yourself this. If God did not discourage it, then why does the church?" Petra and Jesus looked at each, searching for rebuttals, but stayed silent.

Fernando knew that he would probably not have this opportunity to fully explain their situation to them again so he decided to lay it all out on the table. He continued, "As you know, I grew up Catholic. My mom and I attended almost every mass we could when I grew up. But never once did I ever hear anyone talk about the subject."

"You mean polygamy?" Jesus said scathingly.

"Well, the correct term for what we are considering is Polygyny. Polygamy is the whole thing wrapped into one. A man who marries more than one woman, a woman who marries more than one man. But polygyny is where a man has more than one wife. Polyandry is where a woman has more than one husband. We prefer to describe what we're considering to be just plural marriage. Just adding someone to our existing marriage. But some religions have taken this, which was just a simple way of life, and turned it around to benefit the men and empower them over the women of their faith. Some people are even taught that by taking several wives, they would find salvation or favor by God. In my opinion, religion really shouldn't have anything to do with it."

"One of the biggest misconceptions is to believe that polygyny was invented by a particular religion, when in fact it wasn't. It was just a way of life that some people in the Bible chose to live. To label that it is "a sin" is to make your own conclusion simply because it is not a common practice today. God never punished anyone for doing so, nor are there any commandments that say not to do it."

Fernando knew that he would never convince them what they were doing was okay, but he wanted to let them know that they did their research on the subject before diving in the shallow end of a pool. He further explained the government's take on why it should be considered illegal. It was not because it was immoral or wrong but because they didn't want to find a way to tax it. But the most important thing that Fernando and Paulina wanted to convey to them was that they all loved each other, and that nothing would interfere with their lifelong plans.

Hours passed before Jesus finally agreed to allow them to stay for the night as they had intended, but that they should leave first thing in the morning.

Everyone went to bed but no one seemed to get any sleep that night. Paulina and Celina decided to pack so that they could get a jump-start on their trip home. Fernando rested as best he could because he knew he had a long drive ahead of him.

The next day they made their way home, not speaking too much for the first couple hours. Celina was gazing solemnly out of the window. Paulina turned to her and asked if she was okay. Celina shrugged her shoulders miserably without answering.

What was troubling Celina the most was how she had been plotting behind their backs to get back with Jaime. But now it was clearer than ever before what she really wanted. She wanted to pursue a life with them. She just knew that once he got out of prison, he would do everything he could to interfere and disrupt everything they had and would never leave her alone. She couldn't find the courage to tell them what she had done.

"I'm fine," she said after a few moments. "I really love you guys."

"We love you, too, Celina," Paulina replied. "Don't worry about what my dad said. He's just old fashioned. He'll come around."

"He said he was going to cut you from his will if you didn't stop doing this," Celina worried.

"He said the same thing when we told them we were going to get married. His bark is much harsher than his bite," Fernando interjected.

"Heck, the truth is, I wouldn't know what to say if I were him and my daughter told me that's what she wanted to do," he said laughing.

CHAPTER THIRTEEN

The Big Show

The next few days were hectic. They were all trying to make all the final preparations for Celina's artistic debut. Not a stone was left unturned. Everyone was ready. Celina would finally have the exposure most artists would die for. The night before the show, they stayed up late trying to relax and get their minds off of what was sure to be a rip-roaring weekend. They played a game of Texas Hold'em the night before and drank a bottle of wine Fernando had taken from Jesus' cellar just before all hell broke loose.

"So," Celina said inquisitively. "So...tell me more about this whole asking me to marry you guys thing," she said glowing with an oversized smile.

Fernando and Paulina were unprepared and bewildered how to respond. Paulina stumbled a response and signaled Fernando to go and get something out of their room. Fernando quietly made his way to the bedroom closet while Paulina explained their intentions.

"Well, Fernando and I were thinking..." she said sensitively as Fernando re-entered the room. She looked at Fernando and motioned a nod toward Celina. Fernando kneeled in front of Celina and clasped her hand in his. They could feel the temperature rise from each other's hands as Celina started to fidget. Her grey sweatpants wouldn't stop shaking because she couldn't control her knees from trembling and her eyes began to fill with tears.

"Celina," Fernando began to speak, "I never dreamed in a million years we would all one day be like this. Meeting you was one of the greatest things that have ever happened to us. We love you. And we want to express that feeling to you by asking you to marry us." Fernando pulled a one-carat diamond ring from behind his back and asked, "Will you marry us?"

Celina waited a few seconds before saying breathlessly, "YES! I love you guys so much."

Still on his knees, Fernando placed the ring on her finger while Paulina stood beside him and watched him propose. She could not fight back her tears that trickled down her face as she held her hands over her heart.

Everyone embraced exchanging affections before they made their way into the bedroom to consummate their engagement.

The next morning the sun cracked through the windows warming Celina's face. She stretched out her arms and turned to her side only to find that her fiancés were not there. They had awakened before her allowing her to catch a few more z's to prepare for her day. She took a long hot shower rinsing away all that seemed to be troubling her just hours before, then dried off, and decided what to wear.

Paulina was at the breakfast table drinking coffee and polishing off the breakfast burritos that Anita prepared for them. Fernando was reading through the paper, trying to find the ad he ran about the show that day.

"Good morning ya'll," Celina said as she made her way down the stairs still brushing her dark curly hair.

"Ya'll?" Fernando replied. "Sounds like you're a Texan there little lady," he said leaning forward to kiss her good morning.

"Today is going to be a terrific day," Celina exhaled as she opened her arms towards Paulina.

"Yes, it is sweetie!" Paulina told her attempting to hand her a cup of coffee and hugging her with her free arm. "We have a busy day ahead of us so we should probably start heading out now."

"Yes we do," Celina said grabbing herself a homemade burrito. With her mouth full of bacon, egg and cheese, Celina muffled out, "Let's go!"

Back at the gallery, the twins arrived to find the wine caterers waiting on them along with Christina who had forgotten her keys again.

"Oh my God, am I glad to see you guys," Christie said.

Rushing out of the van with keys in hand, Alex asked her if they had been waiting long or if they had just arrived.

"They were here when I got here. I stayed up late last night studying so I was running a little late."

"Sure you were up studying," Eric slowly said grinning. "Were you taking the "Bar" exam?"

Giggling, she nudged his shoulder and whispered "Don't tell Paulina okay?"

A short while later Fernando, Paulina and Celina arrived in their Mercedes and could quickly tell how busy they would be by all the hustle and bustle inside. Everyone seemed to know exactly what to do and that gave each the first sign that this was going to be an event of a lifetime.

They spent the morning preparing for the show, which would be held after normal business hours. The place was immaculate and everything looked elegant. Just the way the three of them had dreamed. Nothing could stop them now, not even a tornado— which that part of Texas was used to getting.

The day seemed to drag on while waiting for guests to arrive. Finally just before the show began, a reporter from the Fort Worth Star-telegram walked in. He was a tall and heavy- set man who wore an untied purple tie and breathed heavily when he spoke.

"Hi. I'm looking for Fernando De la Mar," he said to Christie showing him his press pass.

"Sure. I'll go and get him for you. Please, help yourself to the bar."

"Thank you, darling. That would be wonderful."

Christie, bothered by the gentleman, advised Paulina there was a man from the paper here to see Fernando.

"Tell him he'll be right with him," she instructed Christie. Paulina went to snap up her husband who was in the middle of speaking to another guest with Celina.

"Jim Maxwell is here to see you," she charmingly told her husband.

"I'm sorry, who?" Fernando asked

"James Maxwell. The reporter," she forewarned him.

"Excuse us," he said to his guest as he and Paulina walked to one off the bars where he stood. "Isn't he the guy who gave us a bad review when we opened this place?"

"Yes, he is," Paulina said faking a smile as they approached him.

"Jim. What a pleasant surprise," extending his hand to shake his. It's been a long time. How are you?"

"Not as good as you, it seems these days. Looks like you're doing well for yourself, I might add. You know, I must say. Not too many people surprise me. But you on the other hand did a lot better than I ever expected opening this place. You've come a long way."

"Well, thank you Jim. Coming from you that's quite a compliment," he said graciously hinting of arrogance. "I didn't expect to see you here."

"Well, when I heard of the show you were having, horses couldn't drag me away."

That's about the only thing that could, Fernando thought to himself.

"So tell me, who's this girl your having all this for and how did this all come about?" he began to inquire. "She's from New York is that right?"

"Well, yes she is. By way of Brazil," he added. Fernando signaled Celina who was entertaining the other guests who were starting to arrive, to come over.

"Celina Santa Cruz, I'd like to introduce you to James Maxwell. James is a reporter from the Fort Worth Star-Telegram.

"It's a real pleasure to meet you, James," Celina said as she firmly grasped his hands.

"The pleasure is all mine," he said as he made eyes at her. Please, call me Jim."

"Jim was kind enough to give us our first real review when we opened De La Mar Gallery many years ago. Simple and unvarnished were the words I think you used to describe us, wasn't it?"

"Now, now, Fernando. Let's not get impudent here. My compliments for what you've done so far. But now let's focus our attention on your new prodigy. Tell me, where did you get your start?" he said beginning his queries to Celina.

"Well," Celina said clearing her throat. "Where do I begin?"

Just then as Celina took center stage, Fernando got a tap on his shoulder. He turned around to see Andy, his long time friend from jolly old England.

"Andy?" he said wide eyed, "What's going on, buddy?"

Andy wrapped his arms around Fernando not caring to crinkle his new suit.

"Fernando, you son of a bitch. How the hell are you?" Andy was never one to care about glitz and glamour and was definitely not one to consider his audience.

"What's this then? An entire art show on behalf of Celina? The girl I introduced you to in New York? Where is that old hag anyways?"

He looked passed Fernando and over a crowd of people that now filled the room.

"Keep it down man. That's her behind me." Celina was trying to nonchalantly walk away from them.

"What? Celina! He said yelling past Fernando. "Is that you? My, you look ravishing. Come here, give us a hug."

"Andy! It's so nice to see you! How have you been?"

"Not as good as you, love. Why haven't you given us a bell?"

She lowered her eyebrows and turned her head before say "I'm sorry? Bell?"

"Why haven't you called me," rolling his eyes smiling.

"Well I...," Fernando interrupted them and said, "Celina was just about to do an informal interview with our guest from one of our local papers Mr. Maxwell."

"Oh, hiya. I'm Andy," he said nodding his head to him. "So, where can I find some pub grub around here? I could eat a horse. I know you were thinking the same thing weren't you?" looking at Jim suggestively. "I bet you could fancy some nosh right about now, couldn't you?"

At that time Fernando had no choice but to leave Celina alone with Mr. Maxwell to finish speaking to him.

"Well, we'll leave you two alone to finish talking. I'm going to get my friend here something to eat."

Fernando reluctantly left Celina behind while he and Andy went near the front of the gallery.

"So what's been going on, Fern? I haven't spoken to you since you left New York about half a year now," he poked at Fernando. "So I see you two hit it off well then, yeah?"

"Funny you mentioned that, man," Fernando began to explain. "Okay, so I'm going to tell you something, but you have to promise me you're not going to overreact," pointing his finger at him. Quickly looking over both his shoulders he whispered "We're engaged."

Nearly choking over his glass of wine he grabbed from the bar he replied "What? You've got to be joking mate? You left your wife? Are you off your trolley?"

"No, you moron. We're engaged," motioning his hand in a circle. "Me, Paulina and Celina."

"I don't get it," he said confused. "Did I miss something?"

"Paulina and I have decided to enter into a plural marriage with Celina. I proposed to her last night" he said so proudly. We haven't decided on a date yet but I'm thinking in another couple of months or so. You should come." he advised Andy who was still in disbelief.

"Oh, okay, that's great then. My friend's a polygamist. Cheers," he said as he lifted his glass sarcastically.

"Keep it down would you? I don't want anyone to know. Besides, it's not like what you probably think. We didn't join some weird religion or a part of a cult or something. We just fell in love with each other and decided to make it official."

By that time the room was packed full of people so Fernando asked him to stand nearby while he made his rounds. Andy was dumbfounded at the idea of the three of them hooking up like that and yet in good old Andy fashion, was thrilled with it at the same time.

As Fernando began making small talk to an art collector from Dallas, he noticed yet another familiar face in the crowd. It was Jessica, Celina's friend from New York. Jessica was dressed in a semi-formal gown that really showed off her form and was draped softly against her toes. Having only met her once, there was no mistaking her among the crowd. He stopped at the bar where he asked Eric for a glass of champagne before making his way to greet her.

"Hello there," he so charmingly said. "You probably don't remember me, but we met..."

"Fernando right?" she asked him abruptly.

"That's right. We met outside that art gallery in the village. How have you been?" he said as he handed her a glass of bubbly.

"Just fine," she stammered her reply. "So where is Celina? Isn't she here?"

"Yes she is. Oh my God, yes she is!" realizing that Celina has just spent the past twenty minutes with Mr. Maxwell. "Come on, I'll take you to her."

He took Jessica by the hand and started to make his way to Celina, passing up several people who wanted to say hello to him. He just kept moving forward hoping Celina didn't reveal too much to Mr. Maxwell.

He found Mr. Maxwell standing with a group of art dealers who were discussing some of the pieces on display when Jim said "Fernando, You've got yourself quite a girl there."

"I'm sorry? What? What do you mean?" he said thrown off.

"Celina. She's quite gifted," he said, complimenting her. "And oh, don't worry; she didn't stay long talking to me. Your beautiful wife came by and pulled her away while you were gone."

Relieved, Fernando wheezed out a quiet thank you under his breath to Paulina. He looked over to the back of the room and saw that Celina was engaged in conversation with one of the editors of D Magazine from Dallas.

"Well, I'm sorry to hear that, Jim" he said with an iniquitous smile. "Hopefully you can write a good enough review about us this go around. I'm sure you guys can speak again some other time."

"Oh, you can count on that Fernando. So, tell me, Celina said that she was living with you out at the Long Branch. Is that right?"

Fernando's smile dropped as he stood there speechless as Jessica in continuous order, said, "Hi, I'm Jessica" extending her hand to Mr. Maxwell.

Unconcerned he replied "Hi, it's nice to meet you." Then turning his interest back to Fernando and reiterated "Fernando, is it true? Is she staying with you and your wife in your home?"

He had always prided himself for being honest in all of his affairs, but he felt it best he didn't say anything that could jeopardize his business or his family. He looked at Mr. Maxwell in the eye and said "I don't see how that is relevant to anything," trying to avoid the question. Jessica stood their looking back and forth at them like watching a tennis match.

"Well, I just find it interesting that she is staying with you that's all. Is she related to you?"

"Jim, I really don't see how this is important. Why don't you have a look around at all of her work so that you can write a better review? That is why you're here, isn't it? To write a review?" he asked apprehensively.

Laughingly and knowing he had gotten under Fernando's skin, he reminded Fernando that he was a reporter. And reporting what the people deserved to know, was exactly what he was going to do.

Taking the hint he had given, Fernando excused the two of them and went over to Celina and his wife. Celina was clearly living in the moment and was innocently incognizant of people like Mr. Maxwell. He looked at Celina who was having the time of her life. Surrounded by people who were there just to see her and admire her work. He decided not to say anything about what had just happened.

Coming from behind her, he kindly interrupted and said "Excuse me everyone. Celina I have a surprise for you," he gently nudged Jessica in front of him only to have Celina scream in surprise "JESSICA!"

"Oh my God, I can't believe you're really here," she said falling into tears. Everything seemed to be falling right into place for Celina. She had all she ever wanted in life. "I'm so happy right now. I don't know how to act."

"I wouldn't have missed it for the world," Jessica said as she hugged her. "I've missed you so much."

"I am so glad you remembered. I thought you weren't going to be able to make it. When did you get in town?" Celina inquired.

"Just a few hours ago."

Fernando motioned to Paulina to come near him so that they could talk. Seeing there was something troubling her husband, Paulina slowly walked towards him when Fernando said, "We have to talk."

Fernando turned to the girls and told them he was going to let them catch up and that they were going to mingle.

Fernando walked with Paulina to another area of the room and with his hands in his pocket; her told her what Celina had advised Mr. Maxwell. Paulina tried to encourage Fernando not to concern himself about it and that there was nothing to worry about, until there was something to worry about.

Meanwhile, Andy joined Celina and Jessica, and they began to catch up on old times. That gave the De la Mar's a chance to gauge how well the event was doing. It seems as though everyone whom they had invited—attended.

Sales were up, too. Christie had estimated to Fernando that about 250 guests have arrived so far. Paulina also informed him that a couple from Phoenix, Arizona scooped up all three of Celina's paintings that were in the rear of the studio. Another couple was also asking about "Sky Rider" the oversized Indian sculpture that was outside the gallery that first caught Fernando's eye.

Scanning the crowd, Fernando saw his mother Maria, his brother Joe, and his sister Rosalinda and her husband Pete. They all lived nearby and were very close to Fernando, but he didn't get to see them that often as life would have it. His mother was very proud of Fernando considering since his father's death, she always had to work two jobs to support her family but constantly encouraged her children to pursue their dreams. By comparison, Fernando was the one who went above and beyond the call of duty when it came to his education. His brother Joe graduated high school then soon after landed a job as a factory worker where he was now running the warehouse today.

Rosalinda, who he calls Rosie, had married her high school sweetheart after graduation and began having children soon after that.

They were just average middle class people who all looked up to Fernando and all his accomplishments. They all came to offer their brother and sister-in-law support and to meet Celina whom they knew little about.

"Mom," Fernando called. "Over here. I'm glad you made it," he said giving her a hug. "Hey bro. What's up?" Fernando smiled at his brother.

"Hey Fern," Rosalinda reached out to him. "You remember, Pete," she said of her husband. "Where is Paulina?"

"She's around here somewhere" he paused to take a look at his family. "Man it's good to see you guys. I'm so glad you all could make it. So what do ya'll think? Nice huh?

"Yeah bro! You went all out. Then rubber necking the bar, Joe asked his brother, "Hey man, "Is that free beer over there?"

"Yeah man. Help yourself," he encouraged. "Bring me one too while you're at it."

Fernando was pleased that he had his family there to celebrate this wonderful occasion with him. Family profoundly enriched his spirit because it was the single most important thing in his life.

Consequently, it was one of the reasons why he could extend his love and devotion to another woman besides his wife. He knew that love is limitless and timeless. He felt he had a right to fall in love with whomever he pleased, because there was nothing wrong with sharing his love with someone worthy of having it. He knew that he could equally share his heart with more than just one person and not retract in position his love and commitment to Paulina.

When his brother came back he immediately wanted to introduce them to Celina. He walked them across the room where Celina was explaining some figurines she had made of horsehair to some locals. At the first opportunity, he introduced her to his family.

"Celina, this is my family," he said proudly. He introduced them one by one, and she gracefully kissed each of them on the cheek and gave them a warm welcome. They immediately took to her charms and reciprocated pleasantries. Joe, who was not that much older than Celina especially thought she was not only talented and gifted as an artist, but also very attractive. She was someone he wouldn't mind getting to know on a more personal level.

He thought he might have a chance to get to know her better if he were to ask her out on a date. At every opportunity he made it known he was interested in her by telling her how smart and talented she was and how much he admired her work and things of that nature.

Joe later turned to his older brother and leaned up to ask him in his ear if she were single. Fernando wasted no time telling him that she was already spoken for by someone else in the business, and that he should just leave her be before he found out.

Celina, on the other hand, took to Fernando's mother dearly that night. Maybe because she reminded her of her own mother. Celina seemed to block everything that was going on for a short while and focused on every little detail of Maria. The way she looked at her when she spoke and the soft melody of her voice. The way her dress draped across her corpulent figure that still had the hanger marks on it as though it had not been taken out of the closet for a while. She noticed the slight scuffmarks on her black leather shoes with inappreciably worn soles. She appreciated the pseudo gold jewelry that she was sure she had carefully selected to wear that night. To that point, nothing about moving to Texas had impressed Celina more than meeting Fernando's mother for the first time.

Maria never allowed Fernando to spoil her with fancy gifts or lavish her with unnecessary worldly treasures. She would tell him that his success was the greatest gift he could give her and if he wanted to bless her, he should bless his brother and sister by making sure they didn't go without. What made Maria happy was that she knew that her children were happy. Nothing more.

As the evening was drawing to an end, Fernando and Paulina invited them over to their house for a backyard barbeque the following weekend. They kindly accepted, then bid their goodnights, and wished them continued success and happiness. As they left, Celina told Fernando what a pleasant surprise it was to meet all of them and how pure in heart they all were.

As she was telling Fernando how she felt, Jessica couldn't help but notice how Celina was acting about something as simple as meeting his family. She had a peculiar look on her face as she watched the two of them interact towards each other with Paulina not giving it a second thought. Jessica elected not to say anything to Celina about it that night until she could have more of a one-on-one with her.

As the crowd began to disperse, Andy, who by now had a few drinks in him, asked Fernando if they could have a word.

"So what's all this? You and Celina are shagging now? I would have never guessed she was a slapper, old chum. How is she in the sack?"

"Dude, be careful. That's my fiancé you're talking about. Besides, it not like that. We really do love each other," he made clear.

"Alright, put a sock in it, mate. You don't have to get all twisted," he said politely. "How did this all come about?"

Fernando went on to explain what all had happened between them over the last few months while Andy stood there listening in disbelief muffling out an occasional belch now and then. Fernando explained that after she moved in, they began to have feelings for one another and how things just grew from there. He also disclosed how they were forced to tell Paulina's mother and father, and how well that went.

Little did they know, Mr. Maxwell sat behind them listening to every detail of their conversation. He decided he had enough low down on the show to begin writing his review. So he, in an inaudible fashion, disappeared into the night and headed straight to work so that his reassessment on what had happened that evening could hit the morning paper.

CHAPTER FOURTEEN

Coming Out

The show finally closed and everyone was exhausted. They cleaned up a little bit and decided to head home for some much needed rest. Andy and Jessica also went to stay the night at their home at Paulina and Fernando's invitation so that they would not have to spend any money on a hotel. The next morning Fernando went outside to grab his morning paper as he usually did before having his morning coffee. He put the paper down on the table and watched as Anita made them breakfast, telling her of their two other guests. She made small talk to him asking how the night went and Fernando boastfully told her what a success the show had been.

Soon, they all joined him in the kitchen and began to serve themselves with something to eat. Fernando opened up the paper and turned straight to the entertainment section to find Mr. Maxwell's assessment of the show. Fernando nearly choked on his coffee at the headline that read, "Polygamist artist makes Debut."

Fernando was outraged. "WHAT? How dare that son of a bitch do this to us!"

Everyone looked at Fernando puzzled what he could be ranting about. They looked at each other in shock. "What's wrong?" Paulina asked.

"Jim! That's what wrong. Take a look at this," giving her the paper.

With her eyebrows up she read the caption.

"Well, it's out in the open now," Fernando elucidated to his friends. "Damn it! I didn't want it to be like this. No one is going to understand!"

"Understand what? What's out in the open?" Jessica inquired totally confused.

Jessica read over Paulina's shoulder what the paper said about the big show and couldn't believe it either. Celina had never explained to her what they had been doing, but quickly came up with her own culmination of what her friend had been up to, based on what she just saw.

"Is it true? Looking at Celina. "Are you this guy's polygamist? She waited for an answer. "Celina, is it true?"

"Not exactly," Celina replied discombobulated to what was going on.

Just then the phone began to ring. It was Fernando's mother.

"And so it begins," Andy chuckled sipping his cup of coffee.

"Don't answer it," Fernando declared. "I am not in the mood to be chastised by my mother right now."

Fernando thought to himself how all his life, he always tried to do the right thing. Making good judgments and following his heart. But he knew that this was too sensitive a matter for people to grasp without fully understanding its root nature.

Paulina tried to defuse the situation by informing her husband that the article did not necessarily portray the show in a negative light, but it did mention how they all lived together and of their plans to marry one another.

"How in the hell could he have known about any of this?" Fernando placed is hands on his hips and asked. "Was it you Celina? Did you say anything to him about this? What all did you tell him?" he said in a strong demanding voice.

She began to tear up and said, "He just asked me about my art work and stuff."

"Didn't you tell him that we were living together? He told me you did. I knew I shouldn't have left you alone with him."

"Hey, don't yell at her. You guys *are* living together. It's not her fault all of this happened. What did you expect her to say about where she's been living all this while?" Jessica interjected trying to defend her friend.

Paulina gave Jessica piercing look and warned, "Well, don't you come at him like that either. He's my husband, and if anyone is going to jump his ass about it, it's going to be me!"

Paulina turned her frustration to Fernando and said, "She's right, though Fern. You can't be angry with Celina for telling him what she told him. For all we know, he could have overheard you telling Andy about it."

Coming to his senses he apologized to everyone for over reacting and tried to come to terms with what had happened. In a calm and gentler voice, he made it clear that he just wanted what was best for them and didn't want anyone or anything to come between them.

"I love both of you," he added.

"We love you, too" Paulina assured him. "But you can't go flying off the handle every time someone says something negative about us and our decision. We know that what we are doing isn't wrong and together we'll overcome this. I mean let's face it, people are going to say and do a lot of things to try and rationalize why it's wrong and make it seem that what we are doing is against God's will. And against the law, for that matter. But we have to support each other and stay strong for our family. Okay?"

But Jessica was not finished saying what she wanted to say.

"Oh, come on!" Jessica added. "You don't honestly believe that people are going to be okay with it just because you say you love each other. No matter how you try to explain what you're doing, nobody is going to be on board with it. You all can be sure people are going to come against you hard. Are you sure you're prepared for what's next?"

"We are not trying to convert anyone," Celina advised her friend. What we do in our house shouldn't be anyone's business. We're not telling people how they should live their lives so no one should have the right to tell us how to live ours. People can either accept us or reject us."

"That's right" Paulina confirmed. "Nobody gives it a second thought if a woman has five kids from five different men and isn't married to any of them. And of course vice versa. In fact, the government and the church as well as the community will even offer them assistance. We're not asking anything from anyone."

Things began to heat back up as Jessica continued making her point. "Then why doesn't anyone practice it besides those fundamentalist from Utah?"

"Well, that's the real question isn't it? Why? Why doesn't anyone practice it?" Fernando asked.

Andy put his two cents in when he said, "It was probably some good looking woman from a long time ago who, when some guy asked her to marry him, told him the only way she would be his wife was if he would only marry her. Then she probably bragged to all her friends how she made him do it, and then many other women did the same.

"Yeah, imagine if Cleopatra told Marc Anthony, 'Okay I'll marry you but you cannot have more than one wife.' He probably would have said ok just so he could have her."

"Alright, ya'll. That's enough," Fernando said. Let's talk about something else. "We'll deal with that article later." Fernando's phone rang again, and to no one's surprise, it was his mother. He went upstairs to speak to her in private about the whole ordeal. He had to come clean what their intentions were, and predictably, she was not fully on board with it. He ended the conversation with her, however, still extending his invitation for her and the rest of his family to join them on Saturday for dinner. She agreed and told them she wanted to speak more about this to them later.

A week passed, and Andy and Jessica were back home in New York still shaken about what their friends were getting themselves into. Meanwhile Fernando, Paulina and Celina started to experience the wrath of what was in store for them. They received several calls at the gallery from people who questioned what they had read in the paper. They all had agreed to respond with "No Comment" to anyone who would inquire about their social status.

Fernando even spoke with his lawyer on the matter, asking what the repercussions were if they decided to pursue their idea of plural marriage. His lawyer advised him that in Texas, a person could not legally marry more than one person at a time and that even the implication of marriage to someone other than whom you are married, would be considered a second degree felony.

He advised him to look at Texas penal code section 25-01 for more information and further advised him not to have such a ceremony because if found guilty, he could be charged with the crime of bigamy. Those two words stuck in Fernando's mind like thorns. Crime. Bigamy. How could loving someone and wanting to give them a better life be a crime worthy of punishment? Texas penal code section 25-01 must be extremely antiquated, Fernando thought to himself. He decided not to mention this to Paulina or Celina. They had enough to worry about getting all of the wedding arrangements in order. They didn't need to be concerned with the legal technicalities or red tape behind the scenes for their wedding contract. Besides, Fernando thought arrogantly, I can afford to hire an attorney to worry about that stuff and straighten it out for us, if the need arises.

He smiled confidently and said to his attorney, "Well, we will cross that bridge when we get to it."

In the meanwhile, the women decided to split days of the week as to who would have Fernando to themselves. Paulina invited Celina into the living room one night to drink some hot tea and to share some muffins that Anita had left for them.

Paulina informed her that she worked out a way that they could spend time equally with Fernando. Paulina wanted this for Celina—to allow her more one-on-one time with Fernando. She felt that it wasn't fair that they didn't have any alone time together and didn't want Celina to feel uncomfortable having to ask. The idea came to her one night when Paulina looked up successful plural marriage relationships and wanted to give it a try.

Paulina would have him every Monday, Wednesday and Friday. While Celina would have him Tuesdays, Thursdays and Saturdays, and they would all be together on Sundays as they declared that day "family night." Some of the household duties could also be distributed, too. What little there were with Anita's help in the house.

The weekend came around, and his family came to the house as expected. They all gathered around the picnic table to dine alfresco. Maria brought the homemade tortillas that Fernando loved so much to go with the fajitas he made out on the grill. Celina made her famous Spanish rice and charo beans that could feed an army. Rosie helped Paulina make some guacamole and pico de gallo, while Pete assisted Fernando out in the back yard. They all sat around the table eating dinner, drinking sangria, and sharing a few laughs exchanging childhood stories.

It was times like this that Fernando loved so much. Fernando felt compelled to stand up and say something.

"I'd like to make a toast," he said tapping his glass with a fork. Looking around the table, he lifted his glass and went on to announce, "I would just like to say that I am very happy to have all of you here with us this weekend. I hope that we can spend many more days like this in the future. Nothing is more important than family."

His eyes began to water as he proudly said "To Family!"

Everyone seemed to be in harmony sharing Fernando's feelings and emotions. But you could feel a faint stiffness rise in the air that came from Fernando's mother who wanted to rekindle their conversation from earlier. She shifted in her seat as though something was bothering her but couldn't bring herself to verbalize what was on her mind. It was her intention however to bring the subject of her son entering into a plural marriage to a close. But she decided to wait until after dinner. She waited until Celina asked if everyone wanted to go inside for desert before asking her questions.

Maria inhaled before saying everything that was on her mind.

"So how does this all work? Have you changed your religious beliefs? Are you sure you're doing this out of love? I mean, I know you and Paulina wanted babies, and Celina is so much younger than you are. Is that why you want to do this?"

Fernando didn't know what to say. He was fast getting worn down from having to explain himself to everyone. But he knew that by having this kind of relationship, he must begin getting used to it.

He gathered his self-possession and began by saying, "Okay, look, Paulina, Celina and I love each other and that's it. We have decided to enter into plural marriage with each other and I expect all of you to be a bit more supportive. Now, I know it is against the grain of everything that you know about marriage up to this point, so I'm not expecting you to be 100 percent receptive, but I do hope that you will understand and will ask me questions about it so that you can try and understand. I don't want to feel uncomfortable speaking to you about it, because the fact is, we are excited about getting married. I just want to know that you have our best interest in mind."

He went on to say "Now, mom, I'm going to try my best to answer your questions as best I can."

"Here's how we think our relationship will work:

1. Celina will live in the house with us—that is, until I can build her a house of her own. We have plenty of space here on the ranch so I don't foresee it being a problem.
2. I am not marrying Celina for any other reason other than we fell in love with her. We want for her to be a part of our lives forever. I'm not marrying her because Paulina and I want to use her as a baby factory. There is nothing wrong with Paulina, and I'm not sure how I feel about you asking us that.
3. As for religion, I hardly even go to church. I wouldn't even consider myself a member of any church right now.

Although, I would like for all of us to find one we can call home in the near future, this is not a religious decision. But my belief in plural marriage is not because some angel came down from heaven and told me to have multiple wives in order to receive celestial favor. I'm marrying Celina for the same reasons I married Paulina. It's simple. Because I fell in love with her and couldn't see spending my life without her."

The room got deathly quiet as Fernando explained to them his position. Then his mother spoke again, and said, "But it's a sin, Fernando. God did not intend for men to marry more than one woman at a time."

Fernando was quick to respond when he said "Where in the bible does it say that it's a sin? Was it a commandment? No. Is there a book or passage in the Bible that says where people were condemned by God, or Jesus, or even a high priest for that matter? No. It does, however, give us plenty of examples of people who in fact did have more than one wife at a time throughout the scriptures."

Still having everyone's full attention, he continued.

"Take a look at King David for example. The Bible says His heart was perfect, and he had seven wives. And, God said that if David wanted more, he would have given him more. If God did not intend for men to have more than one wife, how do you explain this? Plus, he's not the only one in the Bible. Read it for yourself. We all know that people of those times had multiple wives, and yet we think that by doing so today, it's wrong. But why? Why is it wrong?" No one said anything.

Fernando annexed his thoughts with "I even read how in most countries throughout the world today, that women outnumber men three to one. Whether it be because of war, homosexuality or whatever other reason, this is a fact. So if every woman is to have but one husband for herself, how is this possible?

"Wow, man that's deep," Pete said. "I never thought about it that way."

"It's against the law in most states, too, right?" he curiously asked.

With a simple nod of his head, Fernando agreed. "You should, like, go to the capitol and try and change those laws Fern. People will listen to you. In the end, people are suckers for the truth."

Fernando smiled and said, "Man, do you know how much opposition I would face? I don't know about all that, but I would like to say that someone should. I just don't know if that someone is me right now," he added.

"So you're getting married? To Celina, too?" his mother exclaimed.

"That's right, mama," Paulina joined in the conversation. "Show them your ring, Celina."

Celina scooted up from her chair and modestly flashed her one-carat diamond ring.

"That's beautiful," Rosie told Celina. "Congratulations! Who picked it out?" she asked Paulina enthusiastically, "Was it you or my brother?"

"We both did," Paulina told her.

Then Rosie asked her, "So when were you guys thinking of getting married?" as she lightly clasped her husband's hands in hers.

"Six months from now. In the fall" Celina interjected.

"Can you legally get married like that here in Texas?" his brother Joe asked.

Joe was your typical egotistical male who was in no way shape or form one to embrace marriage – of any kind. Joe was a late thirties man who lived alone in a studio apartment in an old converted train depot in downtown Fort Worth. Knowing all of that, Fernando questioned himself if he were legitimately asking because he cared or was it for something more cynical.

"No, you can't" Fernando advised his brother remorsefully. "We will however have a beautiful ceremony and exchange vows just like any other wedding."

Celina added that the plan was to invite friends and family to share their special day with them, and afterwards, have a dance before they rushed off for their honeymoon.

"We were thinking of having it here at the ranch" Paulina said.

The mood began to change favorably as his family began to understand and see for themselves that love was the motivator for their union.

CHAPTER FIFTEEN

Here, Lies, Truth

Weeks went by and the three of them were living in almost perfect harmony. Looking back on Celina's show, though a success, it didn't quite turn out the way they had planned. Art sales were up by almost 30 percent but they knew it would have done better if it were not for the article that was written about them. They encouraged Celina to continue working and try not to let what had happened to them bother her. They promised that everything would eventually turn out just as they had planned.

Celina took their advice and tried to lose herself in her work as they suggested. She put on her favorite pair of jean overalls that were blanketed in different colors of paint and an old smeared Van Halen t-shirt that she got from a vintage music shop back home. She pulled back her hair and turned on her radio to her newly found favorite Spanish station.

Celina had just begun to mix her colors went Paulina gently knocked on her door which Celina had left open.

"Can I come in" Paulina asked.

"Yes, of course, please," Celina said as she turned down the music. "What's up?" Celina asked as she tried to fix herself up.

Paulina admired how Celina could stay focused despite their troubles of dealing with the bad media attention and the picture they began to portray of Celina.

She looked at her in her element for a moment noticing how cute she looked in her outfit. But she reminded herself that she was there to ask Celina something important.

"So, I was thinking," she paused. We have a lot of planning to do if we're going to have this wedding in a few months."

Celina's eyes widened as she couldn't help but smile.

"Oh my God, I was just thinking the same thing. What did you have in mind?" Celina asked.

"I should be asking you that," Paulina countered. "It's your wedding."

"No, it's OUR wedding," Celina contradicted her. "It's just as much you're wedding as it is mine. But thanks for making me feel so special. You don't know what that means to me," she said with her lips pouted outward.

Suddenly another voice snuck up on them. It was Fernando who peaked his head through the door. "Am I interrupting anything?" he asked as he entered the room.

"Yes you are," the girls agreed as they shared a laugh.

"Well, I won't stay long," he assured them. "I just came by to bring you some mail," and handed Celina a letter. It was clearly from an inmate at a local prison. He looked disturbed not knowing what else to say. Paulina shared his perplexity when she noticed how Celina's expression immediately changed.

"So who is that from, if you don't mind me asking," Fernando said.

Her voice cracked as she whimpered and searched for an answer. "Umm, no one important. It's my…aunt's son who I went to see in Austin," she explained as her forehead began to glisten with perspiration. "Yeah, it's from my cousin, Jaime. I hope its okay that I gave him our address?"

Fernando slowly shook his head as if to imply that he didn't mind, but it was clear that thoughts began to enter his mind for the first time on how well he really knew her.

"It's fine, Celina," Paulina assured her. "I think what he means to say is, it would have been better if had you told us first before giving him our address."

Celina's attitude began to change as if she had something to hide. There was no mistaking the appearance of discomfort she had as she began to explain to them. "What? I can't have my family know where I live? Is that what you're telling me?"

"No, Celina, it's not that at all. It's just that we don't know him. Why haven't you mentioned him before?" Paulina wondered and thought to herself that this could not be happening. Her eyebrows lifted waiting for an answer. "Celina…?"

"Look, I don't know, okay? I just didn't," Celina defended her actions by telling them how having a cousin in prison was not something that she was particularly proud of. She quickly began putting away her easel and paintbrushes subtly suggesting to them it was time for them to leave.

Picking up on her hints, Paulina and Fernando reluctantly gave Celina her space still not sure why she didn't understand their point of view. They worked very hard for the things they had and simply did not feel comfortable having a stranger clearly of questionable character knowing where they lived.

Celina immediately opened the letter to find that Jaime had read about what the paper said of her living in a polygamous relationship with the De La Mars. He did not hold back and told her what a whore she had become and what a bitch she was for leading him on. But what disturbed her most was finding out that he had made early parole and would be out in less than six months.

"Oh my God," Celina cried out. "What have I done?" she said as she began to cry aloud.

She laid down in a fetal position on the couch and placed her hands over her head in shame. She had never been more confused and beside herself in her life. Her biggest concern was that she lied to her new family who were only looking out for her, which at the time had seemed like the right thing to do. Her heart instantaneously knew she mishandled the situation, beating as rapidly as it did as she fabricated her story.

She stood up and wiped the tears from her face as if all that had happened was just scuff marks on a pane of glass. She knew she had to come clean with them sooner or later. But she decided on the latter in the hopes that they would dismiss her actions for now and let things get back to normal before breaking the news to them who Jaime was, and what she had been doing.

She decided to wait a day until it was her night with Fernando before mentioning anything to them.

The following night, she and Fernando were getting ready for bed. Fernando stepped out of his slippers and grabbed a book that he had been reading while Celina brushed her hair in front of her small antique vanity.

Fernando had started to read his book by the softly lighted night lamp by the bed tucked away in satin sheets, when he asked her to lie down beside him.

She paused before replying with her rehearsed speech to him, and she began to say, "Fern, we have to talk," putting her thumbnail between her teeth.

"Sure, what's up?" he said, fluffing his pillow behind his back. "Is it about the wedding? Because if it is your better off talking to Paulina about it," he chuckled.

"Not exactly. Look I..." she hesitated nervously. "I want to talk to you more about my cousin. The one in prison."

"Okay," he said feeling confused and beginning to share her nerves.

"He's not my cousin...He's an old boyfriend of mine from back in New York." She waited a moment and noticed how his face went into a distant blank stare over hearing the news of her former boyfriend, who was now in prison.

"Who?" he questioned sliding the sheets from his legs. He sat on the edge of the bed in disbelief running a thousand questions in his head.

"Celina, how...what were you thinking giving him our address?"

Then it dawned on him, "You went to see him, didn't you? When we went to Austin. You did, didn't you?" He stood up from the bed and wrapped his pajama top on looking at her still in shock. He grabbed his cell phone and began to dial.

"Who are you calling?" she asked puzzled.

"Paulina, who do you think?" He did not hide his sarcasm from her.

"I don't understand. Why are you calling her? I thought we could talk about this...alone."

Rolling his eyes, he showed his back to her before saying "Because it involves her, too, that's why. Geeze, Celina how could you?"

Paulina answered and he quickly said, "Hey, hon, I think you need to come over here. Now...Celina has something to tell us."

Only a moment had passed before Paulina, still in her nightgown, came calling. Fernando quickly opened the door seeing her shadow over the window illuminated by the pool. She could tell that something big was stirring by the look on his face and asked what was going on.

"Well, let's have it," he instructed Celina.

Celina came clean with all she had been up to, telling them all about Jaime and their intentions to get back together. She told them how they plotted to live together in the guesthouse until she made enough money to get a place of their own and begin their lives together. Fernando and

Paulina sat there in her small living room listening to Celina tell them her dastardly plan of running away with this man.

"But, that was before all of this," Celina added. "Before we decided to live together as a family. I would not have guessed in a million years I would feel this way about you two. But I love you. Surely you can understand that, can't you? I never meant to hurt you."

She tried her best to assure them she no longer had the same feelings for Jaime like she had in the past, and how they were the best things that had ever happened to her.

"We love you too, Celina," Fernando said. "But you have to understand, too, this has all the makings of getting a whole lot worse once he's out and comes looking for you."

"Wait!" Paulina appealed to him. "We don't know what he's capable of Fern. I mean this is my home. I don't like it one bit that this low life criminal could potentially come around here and do God knows what."

"Look if it makes you feel any better, I'll hire a security company to watch the place when we're gone. Come on, he can't be that stupid," he said trying to set her at ease.

Paulina always felt safe with Fernando. She never had to concern herself with anything remotely close to this before. She trusted him with all her being and knew he would never let anyone harm her.

"I guess."

Still distraught, Paulina said "Well, come on then Fern, let's go to bed," turning away from Celina.

"Wait, hon," he swallowed the lump in his throat. "It's Celina's night," he advised her.

For the first time a sense of discomfort came over them. They looked at each other as though they would never see each other again—that something had been broken. The room was still tense on the matter before them, and Celina knew it was her fault they were all still so worried.

Resignedly, Celina gestured, "You guys go ahead. I'll stay here tonight. You can have my night." She looked at them knowing the trouble she had caused them, but she was offering this as a peace offering to them. Paulina in particular.

Shaking her head, Paulina told her that it wasn't fair for her to do such a thing, and that she should keep her night as they agreed. Fernando watched as Paulina walked out of the room shutting the door behind her.

He wondered if she would ever fully recover from all of this. He knew from experience that gaining Paulina's trust did not come easily and once broken, it was almost impossible to mend.

Fernando took a deep breath and headed toward Celina's bedroom. Images of Celina in bed with another man taunted him. A sneering voice in his head repeated, "You don't know her," as he angrily kicked off his slippers and undressed again. Celina cowered on her side of the bed and waited for Fernando to get under the covers. Instead of lying down, he sat up and reached into his pants pocket for his cigarettes.

"Please don't smoke in here," she said in a voice she hardly recognized, so small and weak. Fernando gave her a stern look and replied coolly, "This is still MY guesthouse and with the way you have treated me and Paulina, I would say you deserve to be treated like a guest." Celina felt a sharp pain as if she had been struck. Fernando had never spoken to her so harshly. She stared at him remorsefully, willing him to meet her gaze so he could see the sorrow in her eyes, but he didn't look at her.

Fighting back tears, Celina rolled onto her side with her back to Fernando. She closed her eyes tightly, praying for some random act of God to happen and make Fernando and Paulina forget what she had confessed to them. But in her heart, she knew she could not keep hiding her past from them or herself. She also realized that it was not Jaime's fault either. She could have cut all ties with him a long time ago.

She rolled onto her other side and attempted to reach for Fernando, but he pulled away from her grasp. He got out of bed and went to the restroom to dispose of his cigarette. After a few minutes, Celina could hear him brushing his teeth. She waited patiently for him to lie back down and whispered, "I'm sorry." "I don't want to talk to you right now," Fernando said firmly. Celina could no longer hold back her tears and began to cry softly as she turned away from him once more.

Fernando listened to her quiet sobbing, forcing himself not to turn around to console her. Every instinct told him to hold her and kiss her, and tell her that he forgave her. His heart ached as he knew Celina hadn't meant to hurt them. But he thought of Paulina, and how heartbroken she must have been, lying in bed alone after listening to something so deceitful from someone she loved.

After about half an hour, he could hear Celina's deep, even breathing and knew she had probably fallen into an exhausted slumber. He gently got out of bed again and quietly made his way to the house, hoping that Paulina was still awake so he could speak with her. To his relief, he could see the light was still on in their master bedroom window. He quickened his pace, as if everything he wanted to say was going to spill out before he could get to her.

Paulina was sitting in their large recliner, holding Fernando's bottle of Scotch, and staring sullenly out of the window. She could hear Fernando's footsteps as he entered their bedroom and without looking up, said, "I saw you sneaking out. What happened?" Fernando stared at Paulina in disbelief, temporarily taken aback at seeing her cradling an entire bottle of Scotch, "Nothing at all. Do you want a glass for that?" he nodded at her lap. "Oh stop it, I haven't drank one drop of it," she said, irritated, "But I wish I could! I wish I could be like so many other people and use this as an escape."

She placed the bottle on the floor and looked at her husband sadly. "How can we trust her? How do we fix this?" she asked. Fernando sat down with her on the recliner and put his arms around her. "I don't know," he answered honestly, "But I do know that I still love her. Don't you?" Paulina nodded her head reluctantly. "She's young and still very naive," Paulina remarked, "But I know she is telling us the truth. It's a tough pill to swallow, but we all make mistakes."

Fernando kissed Paulina on the forehead and asked, "Does this mean you forgive her?" "Yes, but I'm still upset with her," Paulina warned, "Don't expect me to be nice until I've told her exactly how I feel."

Fernando nodded in agreement. "That's fair. I just want to get this behind us. Not that I'm trying to rush you," he added hastily, seeing the look on Paulina's face, "But above all else, we must maintain peace in our home. This is our sanctuary, the only place where we can be our true selves." Paulina raised her face to his and kissed him gently. "I think you need to get back to Celina. I'll be alright now," she reassured him. He smiled at her and said teasingly, "Before I go, would you like me to pour some of that Scotch on your toes and suck it off?"

Paulina looked disgusted for a moment and blurted out, "Yuck! No way, my feet are gross!" Then, as her words sunk in she recanted, "I mean, they're not, but I still don't want you to do that!" Fernando roared with laughter as he headed to their door. "I love you babe. See you in the morning!"

When he returned to the guest house, Fernando was surprised to see Celina awake, crying, and writing furiously on a legal pad. "What are you doing?" Fernando asked in a gentler tone.

"I'm writing a letter," she said angrily.

"To who?"

"Jaime. I'm telling him it's over."

"Celina, you don't have to do that," Fernando stated quietly. "I'm sorry for how we reacted. You told us the truth and we still love you, no matter how much we didn't like hearing what you said."

Celina's face crumpled as she put the legal pad down and reached out for Fernando. He pulled her into his arms and held her firmly until she stopped crying. When she tried to apologize further, he kissed her hungrily on the mouth and began to undress her, whispering to her that it didn't matter.

She kissed him back just as eagerly, her tongue sliding over his lips, letting his hands grope her all over her body. The sudden surge of passion was undeniable. She ushered Fernando onto her small couch and straddled him. As he entered her, she held his face in her hands, never breaking eye contact with him. She wanted him to know that she belonged to him.

"I love you," she moaned as she pushed her hips into his, rocking back and forth in ecstasy. Fernando kissed her hands, arms, neck and breasts. He had intended to be gentle with her, but allowed Celina to take control.

The pace of their love making took an almost frantic turn as Celina felt the waves of her orgasm flood her senses. Fernando gripped her hips firmly as he released himself deep within her and she gasped with pleasure.

They laid on the couch, wrapped in each other's arms, as they fell asleep, not mentioning anything more about Jaime or Celina's foolish plans to be with him.

As the week drew closer to an end, they continued to receive threatening phone calls at work from people who wanted to condemn their home life. Even their co-workers began to look at them differently. Each time they would show up at the gallery, everyone would seem to drop what they were doing and would quietly begin to work pretending they were not there.

Christie pushed the limits one day when Paulina overheard her on the phone with one of her friends telling them about working for "Paulina the Polygamist." It was everything she could do not to fire her on the spot.

So instead, Paulina gave her more duties at work making her go out on deliveries with the twins. She even put blocks on Christie's computer from getting on the Internet as she was so famously known for doing so.

Though only a few months away, no one, up until this point, had made any plans for the wedding. Only this time it was Fernando who decided to bring it to their attention. He took the liberty of hiring a wedding planner.

Around lunchtime, Fernando asked the women into his office for something important he had to tell them. They looked concerned because this was so out of character for him to summon them in such a way. He asked them to have a seat while he went searching his desk for some paperwork. He tossed to each of them some brochures from a company called "I Do Wedding Planners." Their eyes lit up and each let out a sigh of relief as they were overwhelmed with what he had done for them.

"I just want to make sure that you guys have everything you want when we tie the knot this fall," he said, grinning ear to ear.

Childlike, Celina almost gave Paulina an earache when she screamed in excitement, "Yes! Thank you, thank you, thank you!"

Although Paulina shared her excitement; she didn't quite share her enthusiasm. Seeing Celina that excited reminded her of when she and Fernando got married. She was young, sweet, and in love. She didn't have a care in the word, except of course how her parents felt about her getting hitched at such a young age.

Fernando told them that he had invited Rhonda Mae Fields, the owner of I Do Wedding Planners, to come to their house that night for a one-on-one consultation. He also let them off work an hour early to get ready before she came. All he asked of them was not to go way overboard and joked about making sure there was beer and whiskey when it was all over with.

After their impromptu meeting, he stayed behind to finalize their honeymoon trip to Hawaii. He was always full of surprises and thought that would be the perfect getaway for all of them. Paulina had always wanted to go to Hawaii, but they could never find the time to do it due to the huge effort they put into the gallery. Fortunately, he had racked up enough frequent flyer miles that it wouldn't put such a hurt on his pocket book.

Later that evening the doorbell rang, and Celina rushed to answer it. She got up so fast that she nearly walked right out of her shoes.

"Coming!" she shouted trying to slip on her shoes again. She quickly opened their oversized French doors to find a young, vibrant, African American woman standing their holding a white leather portfolio.

"Hi! How are you? Please, come in," said Celina as she greeted Rhonda Mae Fields.

"It is so nice to meet you. What a nice home you have," she said as she gazed at the room. "Who is your decorator?"

"My fiancé actually," she smiled.

"I know, I thought the same thing too," she whispered. Please, have a seat," Celina said, showing her to the living room.

She yelled holding her hand to her mouth, "Paulina! The wedding planner is here!"

Paulina gracefully came down stairs to greet her extending her hand out to hers. "Hi I'm Paulina. And you are?"

"Hi, I'm Rhonda. It's a pleasure meeting you." She was quick to glance over the two ladies who stood before her, but uncertain who the bride was.

"So, Fernando told me just about everything I needed to know except for one thing," she paused. "Who's the bride?"

Paulina and Celina looked at each other knowing this was about to get uncomfortable, waiting for one another to begin to explain. Paulina turned to Rhonda and inhaled a deep breath before saying, "Would you like something to drink?"

"Sure, I'd love that," said Rhonda now more confused than ever.

Luckily, Celina had set out a tray of hors d'oeuvres and a pitcher of sparkling water. They sat down on the couches across from each other as Paulina poured her a glass and told her to help herself to something to snack on.

"Well" Paulina said quizzically, "This may come to a surprise to you but...what do you know about plural marriage?"

Without hesitation, Rhonda replied, "Like when someone marries more than one person?"

The girls squeezed the sofa cushions like a stress ball as they both nodded yes.

"Oh, is this what this is? Great!" she exclaimed. "Momma always said two's better than one! This is going to be better than I thought."

The girls were extremely relieved knowing the hard part was over as they deflated their clasp from the sofa.

"So tell me, what did you girls have in mind? Do you have your colors picked out or are we starting from scratch?"

That's when they realized how little they knew about what each other wanted. Until then, they had not discussed anything specific like that before. Seeing how they were not as prepared as her usual clients, Rhonda opened her portfolio to show them some examples to give them a better idea where to start. She even took out her laptop to show them pictures of weddings she coordinated for other people.

Rhonda also suggested they waste no time in selecting the most important thing they would need, their dresses. She told them she knew of the perfect place where they could go in the nearby City View area of Fort Worth that specialized in custom wedding dresses. Finally things were staring to come together.

CHAPTER SIXTEEN

Face Off

One day as they were at work, everything had seemed finally to have gotten back to normal despite having received unfavorable media attention and the occasional inquiry from nosey patrons. Fernando was taking his weekly inventory when he noticed a man of medium build, with greased-back hair, a white t-shirt, and faded blue jeans walking purposefully towards him.

He approached Fernando and asked almost accusingly "Is this where Celina Santa Cruz works?"

Fernando, taken back at his aggressiveness replied, "Yes, it is. Can I help you?"

"You must be Fernando," the man said, staring Fernando in the eye.

Fernando replied, "Yes I am. You must be Jaime, and Celina doesn't want to see you. I think its best you leave right now."

Jaime sneered at him and stated firmly "I'm not going anywhere until I see her. If I have to come back here or go to your house, she WILL speak to me."

Fernando reached into his pocket for his cell phone to call the police, when Jaime grabbed him by the elbow and whispered fiercely, "Hey man, she belongs to me. And I went away for HER. I'll bet she never told you why either, huh? And it doesn't matter. It's none of your business anyway. Just know that I am NOT going away again unless she comes with me."

Fernando jerked his arm away and said firmly, "She is a part of my family now. And I will do whatever it takes to protect her. Now get the fuck out of here before I call the cops!"

Just then the twins who happened to be in between deliveries, rushed towards them at the suggestion of Paulina who watched through the one way mirror in Fernando's office.

"Is everything ok, Fern? Eric asked waiting permission to wale on the intruder.

"Yes, everything is fine. He was just leaving."

As the twins lead him outside, Alex grabbed him by the arm to which Jaime said, "Get your hands off me," as he shook his grasp off of him. Jaime walked backwards to the front door taking note of Fernando and his guards.

"Okay, Fernando, you win. This time!" he said pointing his finger to him.

"But you may as well let me see her. Because, I'll be back. Either here or at your house. It's up to you," he said as he smirked out the door.

"Who was that, boss?" Eric asked Fernando still amazed with what had just happened. Did you know that guy?"

"Nobody," Fernando said still with adrenaline pumping through his veins.

He asked them to keep an eye out for Jaime to make sure he didn't do anything stupid like mess with anyone's car in the parking lot or throw rocks at the windows. He told them he would be in his office and not to hesitate to call the police if he came back.

Christie was frightened. She hid behind the counter still in shock by the unknown mans actions. Fernando told her not to worry and that everything was under control.

He opened the doors to his office and saw Paulina comforting Celina who was crying in her arms in remorse. Paulina looked at Fernando with fear and confusion asking him what he was going to do about all of this. Fernando checked his wallet for his gun permit then opened the safe to get his side arm.

"It's over," he said trying to reassure them. "He would have to be an idiot to come back. He's not going to risk going back to prison anytime soon."

"But what if he does? What are we going to do?"

"Trust me, he won't," he said as he held them both. "Don't worry. I'll take care of this."

Celina wiped her eyes trying to fight shedding any more tears. She stood back trying to gather her composure before saying how she had no doubt he would be back.

"Ya'll don't know him like I do. He won't give up."

"Have you called the security company liked you promised Fern? I think it's time. The wedding is less than three weeks away," worried Paulina.

"I'll call them right now."

To help ensure their safety, Fernando started to contact security companies to find one that would not only watch over his business but also their home. He was not going to take any chances. He allowed Christie to leave work for the rest of the day with pay and closed up early so that he could take the girls home.

On their way to the house, he stopped at a local gun dealer to pick up some more ammo. He had several guns at home, mostly for hunting, but wanted to make sure he had everything he needed just in case.

The girls were reluctant to go inside with him and told him that he might be overreacting. They said not to do anything irrational like buying a bazooka or something.

Celina had never held a gun in her life much less shot one before. He told them that it would make him feel better if he knew they were protected at all times and to please come inside with him.

He felt it might be a good idea for them to do a little target practice while they were there, since he had his gun with him. He went straight to the counter to a man he had previously bought several guns to say hello.

"Hey, Mr. De La Mar! What can I do you for?" the rusty looking gunsmith asked him as he came from behind the counter.

"Hello, Frank. How are you? It's been a long time," Fernando said, shaking his hand.

"Too long!" he said. "And who do we have here? I didn't know you had any daughters," extending his mitten-like hands to greet them.

"These are my...well, this is my wife Paulina and our close friend, Celina" he introduced them. "I was thinking of getting a new gun for Celina. Like a 9mm or something?"

"I've got just the one you need," nodding a wink at Fernando. He showed it to them letting Celina hold it in her hands for the first time. She gripped it in her hands like a professional and avoided pointing it in anyone's direction.

Frank spent the next few minutes explaining to her how to use it and shared a few more safety tips with her.

"Are you sure this is a good idea, babe?" Paulina whispered her concerns in Fernando's ear. "What are you going to do if he comes to our house?"

Seeing the look of concern on her face, he was reminded that when they were just dating an old girlfriend of his started reaching out to him where he used to work. When Fernando told Paulina what was going on, she met the girlfriend out in the parking lot and ended up punching her in the face after exchanging choice words with one another. The girlfriend never bothered him again.

Fernando smiled at Paulina recollecting in deep wonderment their never-ending love for each other. He kissed her on the forehead as he held her in his arms forgetting where they were until he heard Frank say, "Well, shall we give her a dance?"

"I'm sorry what?

"The 9. Did you want to get it?" Frank said asking for the sale. "I'll even throw in an extra clip for you. What do you say?"

"Yes, we'll take it!"

After completing a background check on Celina, he purchased the gun for her. Picking up a business card for them, Frank encouraged her and Paulina to take a gun safety course together whenever they could.

"Look, this one even offers free breakfast."

They proceeded to try it out in the shooting gallery. As they walked through the narrow hall, the girls trembled at the sounds of the guns shooting off different varieties of rounds. Fernando, steadfast in his desire for them to be proficient with the weapon, encouraged them forward.

He eagerly anticipated watching them shoot as they made their way to the lane. He watched Celina anxiously put on her shooting glasses and ear protection like she had done this before. She took out the weapon from the small metal case and began to load it as she had just been instructed.

Celina told them how she had only seen people shoot guns in movies but always wanted to shoot one herself. She fired off several rounds until Fernando felt comfortable enough with her using it. Then after about an hour, they made their way home.

As they pulled up to the gate, they noticed that someone had disabled the alarm and the gate itself was damaged. It was evident that someone uninvited had tried to enter the home just hours before.

Fernando and Paulina looked at each other in disbelief when Celina asked what was wrong. Fernando clearly disturbed replied "Someone has tried to break in."

"Call the police, Fern!" Paulina said shaken at seeing the dismantled alarm and smashed in gate. She knew that it was pointless to ask the neighbors if they had seen anything since the homes were so spread out from each other. The stone wall that surrounded the setback entrance to the gate provided perfect seclusion and was likely to deafen any noise.

Celina was in the back seat looking around each window to see if anyone was still there but there were no signs of anyone around.

Fernando reached under the seat to pull out his 45 semi automatic handgun in a leather case he had tucked away. He advised Celina to take her new 9 mm out as well—as a precautionary measure.

"Fern, call the cops! Paulina pleaded. "I'm scared." Fernando grabbed his cell phone and called the 911 as he knew to do before going any further towards the house. He explained to them that someone might have tried to break into his home and to send the cops right away.

At the advice of the dispatcher, they stayed in the car near the entrance fearing that someone may be inside. When the cops got there, Fernando told them of the encounter with Celina's ex-boyfriend earlier that day and Celina gave them a full description of Jaime and informed them of his early prison release.

They searched the house inside and out as best they could but suggested to them, if they didn't feel comfortable, to stay the night at a local hotel until the security company Fernando told them about could check the place out thoroughly.

Nothing looked disturbed inside the home as a police officer escorted them around each room looking for any signs of an intruder. They found no evidence of any unwelcome guest inside the home but didn't feel at ease just yet to stay there that night after what had just happened.

The thought of a stranger entering their house uninvited was overwhelming. They each felt clearly victimized in several ways. The house had a strong sense of unease to it that was unexplainable; only a few victims know the eerie feel of a violated place.

Listening to the advice of the police, they all agreed to stay the night in a nearby hotel gathering only what they needed before leaving and taking both vehicles.

No blame was laid on Celina. The damage was done. This was the concern of all three now.

Sharing a double occupancy room, they each settled in, although not able to sleep—wondering when their next run-in with Jaime would be.

Fernando would not stand for anyone disrupting the peace between them—especially the likes of a convicted felon like Jaime. The sun couldn't rise quickly enough. He stayed up most of the night watching TV with the volume turned low, flipping the channels to tune in whatever would take his mind off that dreadful night. Occasionally he would look out the window, imagining catching Jaime in the act of vandalizing their cars or walking the parking lot—then going out there to kick his ass.

But no one knew what Jaime was driving. Fernando also knew Jaime's resources must be limited. He tried to put himself in Jaime's shoes thinking to himself what he would do if the shoe were on the other foot. When the sun finally came up, the light from the window shined warmly on Fernando's face.

With heavy eyes, Fernando woke to find himself laying on a chaise lounge still halfway dressed. He looked over to the beds and saw his two treasures lay there in peaceful sleep. A sharp sense of conviction came over him similar to a lioness protecting her cubs.

He decided to pray, "Lord, I know that I have my faults. And I know that I don't speak to you as much as I should. But I ask you to forgive me for all my sins and protect and watch over us in these troubled times. Please Lord, don't let anything bad happen to them. They are all I have. And I thank you for putting them in my life. I promise to do my part of taking care of them and giving them all of who I am. I put my trust in you dear God, to continue to bless us as you always have. I pray a peace upon Jaime to help him see that Celina has moved on, and for him to do the same. In Jesus name I pray, Amen."

After taking a shower, Fernando quietly got dressed and went to a fast food restaurant to bring them breakfast. Coming back with muffins, pastries and hot coffee, he slipped his key card into the door to see the girls getting dressed.

They were a little upset with him at first for not telling them he was heading out or for not leaving a note. But they quickly forgave him at the sight of the coffee house bags of warm rolls and his handsome smile.

"So what's the plan, babe?" Paulina asked him eating a dainty croissant. "What time are you meeting the security company?"

"Ten o'clock," he said handing Celina a cup of Joe.

"I was thinking we should all take the day off today in light of everything that's going on. Besides, you two can use the off time to make any last minute preparations for the wedding...I'll take care of everything else."

He stole a kiss from them before hitting the road to check on the house.

"So, what do you want to do first?" Celina asked as she grabbed another blueberry muffin.

"Hey I know, let's go and see Rhonda at her salon so we can see how all of the planning is going. Maybe we can find something else we like."

Paulina hesitated before replying, "I've got a better idea." She looked at her future sister-wife.

"But if I tell you, you have to promise not to say anything to Fernando."

"Mum's the word." Zipping her fingers across her lips, Celina childishly sat up on the bed waiting in anticipation to hear what secret Paulina was about to divulge.

"Well, how would you like to go the doctor with me,? she said nervously lacing her lips in her mouth.

Celina immediately thought there was something wrong. Her heart began to race as she sat up from the bed.

"Is everything okay? Are you all right?"

"No, silly, I'm fine. It's just that...Well I've been seeing my doctor about having a baby."

Letting out a sigh of relief, Celina tilted her head back and exhaled.

Then it hit her like a ball to a bat, "Oh my God... Are you pregnant?"

Sadly, Paulina responded shaking her head, "No. Not yet. But she said that everything is normal and there should be no reason for us not to start having kids. Not knowing any of this was going to happen, I scheduled an appointment for today at half past eleven."

Understanding how important it was to Paulina to have a child, she started to share her feelings of excitement. After all, except for those she shared briefly in foster homes, Celina didn't have a big family growing up. She always wanted kids of her own and knew this was one of the things to expect sharing a husband.

Celina swore across her heart not to say a word and went with Paulina to her appointment.

Sitting in the examining room with Paulina stretched out on the table wearing her hospital gown, Celina held her hand. She looked closely at the wall where all the pictures of babies from past deliveries were. She wondered how it would be to one day hold a baby of her own. The doctor, a middle aged Asian woman Mrs. Chan, walked in the room and greeted them kindly.

"Well I have some good news and I have some bad news." They squeezed each other's hands and Celina closed her eyes while Paulina listened intently.

"The bad news is, you're not pregnant yet. The good news is, your hormone levels look good, so you won't need hormonal injections."

She began to explain to Paulina how the results of her last exam came back favorably and not to worry going forward with trying to have a baby. The girls were delighted to hear the doctor tell them the good news.

"I would still like to do some more blood work, just to ensure your hormone levels stay strong when you begin ovulation."

Celina stayed with her while the nurse came in to draw her blood.

"We're in this together," Celina assured her.

Back at the ranch, Fernando showed up to the house just before the security company did. He inspected the gate more carefully and saw for himself what had really happened. He saw how the wires were tampered with and how the alarm was disabled. The wrought iron gate rail was bent forward as if he had pushed them with his car to the point of breaking. Just then, a white van pulled up the dusty road with two uniformed guards. It was the people from the security company he hired. The two men got down from their vehicle and approached Fernando cautiously.

"Hi. I'm Mr. De La Mar and you must be...?"

"Hi I'm Bryan, and this is Dave. We're with First One Security. We understand you had a break in last night?"

Fernando invited them inside to discuss what kind of security would best fit his needs. He also explained to them how not only his house, but also his business, would need full time protection. They were more than accommodating, offering Fernando around the clock security to safeguard his family. Fernando even offered them the guesthouse in the back so that they would have access to a bathroom, a bed and a few amenities.

Bryan took first shift at the house while Dave and Fernando went to go check out the gallery.

On the way there, Fernando received a phone call from Christie who was concerned about a car parked across the street with a man who appeared to be looking in at the gallery through a pair of binoculars. He told her he was on his way there with a security guard and to again and not to hesitate to call the police if she felt threatened.

Dave reminded Fernando that there wasn't anything they could do legally since the man was not showing any intent to harm anyone and that he was perfectly within his rights to park in the street. He also said that he spoke to the police and they did not obtain any foreign fingerprints from the gate nor the house. Without any eyewitnesses, they had no case to pursue prosecution.

Fernando's blood pressure began to boil at the thought of Jaime causing any more problems, because there was no doubt in his mind who the perpetrator was. He started to feel he was dealing with a smarter criminal that he had originally thought. Getting closer to the shop, he knew Jaime's car was facing east, so Fernando decided to drive up behind him slowly just to make sure if it was him or not. Christie had given them a full description of the car he drove so there would be no mistaking it.

Just before pulling up, Fernando pulled in to a nearby gas station where he took out his gun from the glove compartment and showed Dave his concealed handgun permit. Dave, who was also licensed and carrying, assured Fernando that it was not necessary for him to get involved and to just let him handle it. But, Fernando was not going to take any chances.

At a low speed, they drove by where his car should be, but no one was there.

"He must have taken off," Fernando declared.

"This kind of stalker we're dealing with is a creature of habit," Dave explained. "Make no doubt of it, he'll be back."

Just as they were getting out of the car, a black 1988 Oldsmobile cutlass screeched up beside them catching them off guard. Fernando immediately took notice how the front end of the car was clearly damaged.

"Hey Fernando," Jaime shouted arrogantly. "Where's Celina? He smirked.

"And, oh, by the way, how's Paulina?"

Dave held Fernando back from rushing the car. "You son of a bitch! Leave my family alone! Fernando shouted back, pointing his finger at him.

Jaime peeled out of the parking lot, shooting gravel and dust in the air, and laughing at Fernando. He rode off into downtown zigzagging in and out of traffic before disappearing into the distance.

There was no mistaking Fernando's temper. His face turned red with anger as he tried to settle his nerves. Dave advised him not to let his emotions get the better of him, and that it was probably best that he only watch the store during business hours. His number one priority was protecting them at home.

He further explained how his specialty was criminal investigation and surveillance, and he would investigate all the information he could get on Mr. Mata. Fernando finally caught his breath and regained his composure. He decided it was best not to tell Celina or Paulina what happened.

CHAPTER SEVENTEEN

A New Life

It was less than two weeks before the wedding. All of the arrangements for the ceremony had been made, thanks to the creative genius and vision of the wedding planner. All of the misfortunes they had faced seemed to simmer down a bit, and things were beginning to get back to normal. Gifts started to come in from friends and family.

From all but Paulina's mother and father. They told her that they would not be a part of the wedding celebration and didn't want to have anything to do with it.

They told Paulina that neither Fernando nor Celina was welcome in their home and to consider herself lucky to still be in their will. Paulina had a hard time dealing with their decision not to be a part of her wedding but pressed forward hoping that one day—they would come around. She loved her parents very much, and knew they only had her best interest at heart. But in many ways, she felt they were only acting that way towards her so they could continue to control her like they did when she was growing up.

They didn't allow her to have many sleepover's when she was a child for fear that her friends would break something of value. They didn't allow her to date much for fear of her falling in love too young. They didn't allow her to go to the college of her choice, because it didn't fall in with their plans for her.

But when she met Fernando, there was nothing they could do to dissuade her from her love and devotion to this man. And now that she had decided to extend her and Fernando's love to include someone else, there was nothing they could say or do to change her mind.

While Paulina was resting on the couch reading a book, she received a call from an unknown number. She answered the phone "Hello?"

"Hi. Paulina?"

"Yes. Who's calling please?"

"It's me, Angelica. Your cousin from Austin."

Paulina was surprised to receive a phone call from her cousin, because she hadn't heard from her since around the time Paulina got married. It was a pleasant surprise to hear from her cousin, but for a moment, she began to think something must be wrong. The last time she received a call like that, her aunt on her mother's side had died.

"Hi Angelica, it's been a long time. How are you?" She asked uncertain what she might say.

"Oh I'm fine. Just working long hours at the hospital as usual."

"That's right!" replied Paulina. "Momma told me you were a doctor now. The last time we saw each other was at my wedding. I think, and you had just enrolled in medical school at Baylor. Wow, I can't believe it's been that long. So what's going on?"

"Well, my mother spoke to your mother and…" She paused trying to think of the right way to say what she had called for. "I heard you were getting married…again. Is that true?"

Paulina was at a loss for words. She didn't know how to respond. Angelica went into defense mode when she was asked what all she had heard of her engagement. Angelica told her that Paulina's mom and dad went to visit her parents one day, and they told them about her being a polygamist now and how ashamed they were of her for letting Fernando trick her into doing something like that.

"I didn't believe them at first, but remembering how you were always so independent as a teenager and how smart you were, I knew there must be a lot more to it than Fernando making you do something you didn't want to do."

She went on to say, "I did a little bit of research on the subject a couple years ago and learned how in many ways, polygamists were much like the gay community when it comes to some of the suppressions they face and the laws that prohibit them from entering into marital contracts. I read how they may even one day be able to legally marry, but that it will take a little time like it did for same sex partners."

Then Angelica dropped a bomb on Paulina as she told her the real reason why she was so supportive of her and Fernando entering into a plural marriage. She informed her that she was a lesbian and had lived with another woman for the past seven years.

Paulina gasped, "Huh?" unexpectedly and in surprise then said, "Really? Well... Are you happy?"

"Yes very much so. In fact, we were thinking of adopting a baby soon."

"Oh my God! I am so happy for you. So what's your partner's name?"

"Katy," she replied. "We met back in college, and we've been to together ever since."

Luckily, it was Celina's night with Fernando, so they talked on the phone for hours catching up on all they had missed over the years. She explained her plans for the wedding, telling her that only a few select people were invited because of the nature of the ceremony. It was not to be conducted by a minister. Rather, she and Celina would walk down the aisle of the banquet room, one at a time, to Fernando who would be waiting for them at the altar and they would intimately exchange their vows to one another.

"Awe, that sounds so romantic."

Eventually, Paulina extended an invitation to her and Katy to attend the wedding and told her how she would love to introduce them to Celina. Angelica graciously accepted.

Just as Paulina hung up the phone, she heard a loud squeal outside on the patio. As she approached the backdoor, a figure of a man quickly shadowed the window. She let out a scream and called out for Fernando. Hearing his wife's call, he and Celina swiftly got out of bed and rushed downstairs.

Concerned for his wife's well being, he asked, "What's wrong babe? What happened?"

"I just saw a shadow over the window," cleaving herself to him.

Exhaling in relief he reminded her that it was probably either Dave or Bryan who was just monitoring the house. He smiled at her, shaking his head for overreacting, then opened the back door. Chills immediately bolted down his spine to what he saw next. Someone had stabbed one of the dogs to death.

Seeing his reaction, both the women looked over his shoulder and saw one of their dogs lying in a pool of blood. Simultaneously, they both screamed in fear. Fernando tried his best to settle the girls down when their other dog, Bucket, came limping up to them. Celina hurried to call a late night veterinarian while Paulina tried her best to soothe her dog that was in need of medical attention.

Fernando, on the other hand, was furious. For starters, how in the world could this happen? And secondly, where were the guards he hired to watch over them? He stormed out of the house and went straight up to the guesthouse to the make shift command post they had established.

Hearing the banging on the door, they answered to see Fernando in full rage, "What the hell are you guys doing around here?"

"What's wrong, Mr. De La Mar? What happened? They both quickly came outside to find out what was going on.

Nearly in tears of fury and grief over his dog, Fernando told them how someone had just killed one of the Akitas and severely wounded the other. They told Fernando that they had only stepped inside to have something to eat, and so they must have been watched.

Fernando knew that it could be only one person who would do this kind of evil: Jaime.

Dave and Bryan instructed everyone to stay inside while they did a quick search of the perimeter. They circled the house flashing lights on to anything that looked out of the ordinary. They found nothing.

Now they knew firsthand exactly what they were up against and would take no chances going forward to let anything like that happen again.

Of the two guards, Bryan was more reserved, never one to overreact. He always seemed to have a non-expressive look about him; Dave was more impulsive. Quick on the draw, so to speak, and sort of a loose cannon. Having dogs himself, Dave took the animal cruelty personally and vowed to the ladies and Fernando that he would catch whoever did this and would make sure they got what they had coming.

A few days later, they were all at the gallery when lunchtime snuck up on them. The gallery was having a busy day because of a festival that was going on downtown. Crowds of people came in and out of the shop, and no one had time to do anything else but work. Celina's stomach began to growl like a bear when she took it upon herself to leave the gallery alone to go and bring everyone something to eat for lunch.

At her first opportunity, she snuck out the back door so that no one would see her leave. She walked down the street to a nearby sandwich shop hoping to surprise everyone with lunch. She was only there waiting for her order for about ten minutes when she got a gentle tap on her shoulder. It was Jaime.

She was in shock to see him face to face and in the flesh. Her heart began to race as her mind flashed on scenes of what had happened over the last few weeks. He slid across from her in the tiny booth and gazed into her eyes.

"Hello, Celina. How are you?"

"What are you doing here? I don't want to see you." She started to get up. He saw how uncomfortable she was at his presence and pleaded with her to stay and talk to him.

"What happened to us, Celina? Just a few months ago you said you couldn't wait until I got out so we could start our new lives together. Now look at you. Why are you acting this way?"

She told him how she was finally able to see him for who he was, and how she didn't ever want to see him again. "Please Jaime, let me go. Leave me alone."

She went to the counter to get their lunch and Jaime followed her, confused with emotions, holding his hands to his head and pacing the floor. As she opened the door to leave the shop, he hurried behind her and followed her outside. Her pace began to quicken trying to get back to the gallery, which was only a few yards away. She dropped her bag of food as he grabbed her by the arm and spun her around. His attitude had changed like a light switch turning off, then on again.

"Listen to me, Celina, you can't hide from me. I'm not going to let you just throw all we had away like this," he shouted putting both his hands on her shoulders and shaking her.

"It's that Fernando cat, isn't it? He's brain washed you! Don't you see?"

"Let me go! Let me go!" She ran back to the gallery flinging the door open hysterically.

She zipped by customers, and headed straight to the back room. Dave saw her and knew something was wrong. He walked to the front of the store on to the sidewalk to see if what he thought was true. He looked down the street and saw a man who fit Jaime's description walking across the street and getting in to the car he knew to be Jaime's. He immediately called Bryan for back up, but by the time Bryan got to the front of the store, Jaime had made his getaway once again.

Celina locked herself in Fernando's office watching through the one-way mirror to see if she had been followed. Suddenly someone knocked on the door. It was Alex.

"Celina. Are you okay?"

Still trembling, she waited, hearing Alex call out to her a few more times before answering.

"Yes, I'm okay. Can you get Paulina or Fernando please?"

Coming back with both Paulina and Fernando, they all knocked on the door. "Celina, open the door. It's Paulina."

Celina opened the door and began crying, embracing Celina closely. Paulina felt her body shake and caressed her head against her shoulder. "It's okay," she whispered.

"What happened?" Fernando asked. "It was him, wasn't it?"

Celina nodded her head confirming Fernando's suspicions. She went on to relate in detail what had happened, assuring them that he came to her uninvited, fearing that they would think she had something to do with it.

She told them how sorry she was for bringing her troubles upon them like this, and how she would understand if they didn't want to have anything to do with her anymore.

They assured her they did.

With now only a week away from the wedding, it was a perfect, peaceful morning. Andy, who was to be Fernando's best man, called and told Fernando he would be there on Thursday to prepare for the ceremony. In typical Andy fashion, he wanted to know if it was okay if he could bring two of his female companions with him and asked where Fernando wanted to have his bachelor party.

Fernando laughed and said it would be okay if his friends came with him, but that they would have to stay at a hotel while they were there. As for the bachelor party, Fernando was already married so he saw no need to celebrate being single for one last party.

Celina called Jessica and asked if she, too, wouldn't mind coming in a few days early since she had the duties of being her maid of honor. She told her that they had already booked a room for her and not to worry about buying a plane ticket because all of that had already been taken care of. She told her how she could use the company of an old friend and wanted to thank her for not saying, "I told you so" about Jaime.

Paulina found comfort in that her cousin Angelica and her partner Katy were going to join her to celebrate her new life with Celina. She was especially excited because they were also coming in to town early and staying until Saturday night to see them off for their honeymoon.

They had scheduled the wedding to be held downtown at The Omni Hotel. Rhonda wanted everyone to meet her there Thursday evening for an informal dress rehearsal. Everything was going just as the girls had planned. They couldn't ask for anything better.

That night, Angelica and Katy arrived at DFW airport and were immediately impressed at the activity going on at the fourth busiest airport in the world. They rented a small economical car to drive to the ranch, which was about thirty minutes away. When they got there, the soon to be newlyweds, greeted them as they pulled up to the house.

Paulina was thrilled to have her cousin come stay with them and gave Angelica a warm embrace before offering to help her with her luggage.

"It's so good to see you!" Angelica said. She saw Fernando and immediately opened her arms to exchange hugs, giving each other a small kiss on the cheek. "It's been too long, Angelica. I'm so glad you could come."

Celina stood there watching as they got reacquainted, waiting her turn to be introduced.

Katy noticed Celina just standing there ever so eager to say hello, and walked up to her and said, "Hi. You must be Celina? I've heard so much about you."

"Yes, hi. And you must be Angelica's Katy. It's nice to meet you both."

After introductions, everyone assisted them in bringing their luggage inside. They took the grand tour of the home before settling in around the dining room table where Paulina set out a few snacks for them to eat. Fernando, of course, brought out a bottle of wine and began to pour everyone a glass.

"I hope you don't mind chardonnay?"

As the evening turned into night, the atmosphere and conversation began to loosen.

Angelica started, "So, I hope you don't mind me asking but, is this an open relationship or…?"

"No, it's not like that at all," defined Paulina. "We're just your average, everyday people who just enjoy one another. We love Celina, and

Celina loves us. You can just say that we have a "Love Triangle" type of relationship," she laughed.

Arms crossed and eyebrows lifted, her cousin nodded her tilted head and gave a simple smile to Katy who was also listening to Paulina describe their dynamic.

"What? Did you expect us to be having wild orgies and lots of kinky sex?" Fernando said poking fun at his guest.

Everyone began to laugh, and that's when the floor opened to the questions concerning Angelica's relationship with Katy and how that tied in to polygyny.

"No, silly, not at all," Angelica retorted.

"I just wanted to say that I, or we, for that matter, think that it's wonderful when people meet each other, begin to like each other, then fall in love. Isn't that how things ought to be? So simple!"

"That's right, baby," Katy said reaching out to Angelica's clasp. "Angie and I didn't even like each other in the beginning."

"That's right. She and I were paired up on a project in college and well…let's just say we had our difference of opinion when it came to medicine and medical treatment."

"Yeah, but you were so cute when you would try and argue with me and try to tell me what to do. I became intrigued by you and wanted to know more. Before long my curiosity about you and who you were became fascination. That eventually turned to respect and respect in to love. And so on, and so on…" she said as she leaned to kiss Angelica.

"Now, I couldn't see spending my life without her."

"When we heard that you all were going into a plural marriage, we were thrilled to hear the good news. That is a lifestyle very few people, especially here in the states, practice. We believe that if two strong minded people love each other enough and can set any jealousies aside, they can take on the responsibility of an extended relationship and family."

"Paulina," Katy inquired, "May I ask, how do you overcome any jealousies?"

"Well," Paulina answered, "There are many ways. For starters, neither Celina nor Fernando throws anything in my face about what they do when they're alone. Nor I to Celina. And I think it also helped that Celina and I worked out a schedule that defines who spends time with who during the week. Fernando doesn't like to spend much time by himself. I have found that by splitting time with Celina, it gives me more freedom to spend time for myself and likewise with Celina."

"That's right," Celina engaged. "As an artist, I need that time to work on any projects I may be working on so it works out perfectly. Plus, it makes me more appreciative of the time we spend together."

"So, we know about the Rivera family, but have you guys had any people from the public confront you in protest?" Angelica asked.

"Oh yeah," they all agreed.

"And what do you say to people who ask, "How can a man love his wife and share his bed with another woman? Or who say, "How come he gets to have his cake and eat it, too?"

"Well, I say," Fernando volunteered, "That's usually the case in an uncommitted and lustful relationship. But I'm *committing* myself to her as much as I have to Paulina. And vise versa. That's precisely the reason I am marrying her and not just having her around for a lustful and sinful purpose. I wonder what society would say to two women that are content to share the same man. So far it's all been about people who have come against me for this. Why doesn't anyone have the same concerns about them? That alone goes to show how little we know about relationships and what commitment really is."

"It's funny how a family can be ridiculed for plural marriage—thinking it's all about sex. Why couldn't people do polyandry for love? Is that so hard to understand and accept? I feel that I am a better person since I have met Paulina. And you could say, that in so many ways—she saved me."

"In time I hope that people will realize that we did the same for Celina. Taking her out of an unhappy life and giving her a better one. But I guess people would rather that Celina had stayed in a brutal relationship with a man that didn't care for her than to be with two people who would love, protect, and provide for her the way we have."

Then Paulina turned the conversation to Angelica and Katy's relationship. "So what criticisms have you guys faced—other than your parents? I'm sure it's not so different than ours."

Katy took the hot seat. "Well, it was a lot harder in the beginning. But unlike your situation, thankfully the gay community has come a *long* way out of the closet. All though the federal government does not recognize same sex marriage, about twelve states do, so far. And it's become more and more common for people to except gays and lesbians in everyday society nowadays. You see us in movies all the time as well as in the workplace. You even see us on TV shows and listen to us on the radio. In today's society, almost everyone knows someone who is gay, and people are getting more and more comfortable with the idea once they realize we are no different than anyone else. We, too, marry each other out of love, and personally, if we could marry in Texas, we would be married today."

They stayed up all night talking and sharing stories of the similarities between same sex and plural marriage almost until the sun came up.

They all seemed to establish a strong bond for one another as a result of getting to know each other all over again, and yet for the first time. Paulina and her cousin knew that this was only the beginning of a healthy relationship between them, and it was a friendship that they both needed. They would become inseparable.

CHAPTER EIGHTEEN

Undying Love

Fearing she should wouldn't make it on time to her own wedding, Paulina told everyone, "Come on, we're going to be late!"

She rushed them out of the house to meet Rhonda, Jessica, her new boyfriend Paul, and Andy and his friends at the wedding rehearsal. With only two days before the wedding, everyone was beginning to feel the tension that comes with planning such a thing. Though dressed and ready to leave, Fernando was up in his room putting the final touches on his wedding vows. Celina was in her room trying to fix her hair, picking it up then letting it down again, and contemplating cutting it all off.

Angelica and Katy smiled at Paulina as they sat on the couch paying close attention to the clock on the wall.

"Hello?" Paulina yelled up the stairs. "Are ya'll almost ready?" rolling her eyes in frustration. Bryan was going with them just to be on the safe side, having lost a coin toss to Dave as to who would go with them. He followed in his car.

Finally, they all jumped in the Rover and headed downtown to have dinner at the hotel with their friends before practicing who would do what for the wedding.

Fernando nearly broke every traffic violation rushing into the city. He made it just in time to see their friends walking into the elevator in the parking garage. As luck would have it, a parking space was nearby, and it looked like they were not going to be so late after all.

After joining their friends, they ate dinner at an elegant restaurant in the hotel, which was included as a part of the package they chose from the wedding planner. No stone had been left unturned. The wedding was going to be a success.

"We should head to the banquet room so we can do a quick walk-through just to make sure everyone will know where they will be." Rhonda suggested. "Come on I'll show you where it is." As they approached the hall, Bryan stood guard at the door having just given it a run-through. He opened the door to find the room still empty with no tables or chairs yet.

"Okay, everyone" he handed them a paper layout of how the room would look.

"Fernando, you and Andy will be here waiting for your brides to join you. Jessica, you will stand opposite to them also waiting for their arrival. Ladies, you all will walk down an aisle that should be right around here," suggesting a lane with her hands.

"I suggest Paulina coming out first, then Celina. Okay, everyone take your places and I'll start the music I downloaded on my phone."

Everyone took his or her places while Rhonda queued the music. "Okay, just walk normally, people. Not too fast, but not too slow, either. Kind of like this," she said showing them a traditional wedding march.

Those that were not part of the ceremony stood nearby watching as the wedding party did as they were told. They whispered to each other how beautiful it was going to look once the place was decorated—especially Angelica and Katy who were talking about doing something similar to signify their love and commitment to one another.

"Alright, that was great! You did real well. Now, once you exchange your vows and you declare your life as one, Andy will publicly announce you as life partners. Which reminds me, have you thought of a toast for them yet?" she asked doubtfully looking at him.

"As a matter of fact.... I haven't. BUT! I will. After all, I am the one who introduced them," he chuckled. "You lot don't worry about me, I'll think of something to say. You can be sure of it."

As they were all at the hotel, Jaime was alone at a local gentleman's club having a few drinks. He sat at a small round table against the wall sipping on a glass of whiskey, tormented by Celina's rejection. The thought of being without her was too much for him to bear. He did not expect her to move on in such a way, meeting a man like Fernando. The more he drank, his emotions swayed from sadness to anger.

He thought to himself, "How can I compete with a man like him?" But, there was no way he would ever allow someone to steal her from him. He would do whatever it took to get her back and move her to New York.

What he didn't realize, was that Celina was not merely living with Fernando and Paulina in their house. He just thought she might be mixed up in some strange relationship with them. He didn't realize how devoted and committed to the De La Mar's she was—enough to enter into plural marriage with them. A concept he would never understand.

The day before the wedding, Angelica wanted to take Paulina and the rest of the girls for a night on the town since Fernando was going to stay the night with Andy at his hotel room. Nothing too exciting, she just wanted to take her somewhere to listen to some music and have a few drinks to celebrate the night before they got married. Deciding to go to a neighborhood bar, the girls went to let their hair down without the men—promising they would not stay out late.

The men, Fernando, Andy, Jessica's boyfriend, Paul, and Fernando's brother Joe, did the same thing by going to a local sports bar to see a UFC fight. But something seemed to be troubling Fernando. He didn't seem to be having such a good as time as the rest of them were.

His brother Joe asked him "What's wrong, bro? You're supposed to be having fun. Loosen up, man."

"Yeah I know, but I just don't feel that comfortable letting them out alone like that," he said as he shook his head.

The rest of the men joined in conversation. "They'll be okay, Fern. Don't worry so much, man. Jessica will keep a good eye on them making sure they don't do anything stupid," Paul explained.

Andy added, "You worry too much mate. Here have one on me."

"No, that's not it." He played in his mind how to explain to them what has happened the past few weeks with Jaime. He didn't want to ruin the night, but he couldn't keep it a secret any longer.

"Look, the reason I can't relax is because, a former boyfriend of Celina's just came out of prison, and well…"

"Go on. Let's have it Fern," Andy encouraged.

"He's been harassing us at the gallery and stalking us at our home. He even killed one of our dogs at the house."

The men suddenly shared in his concern telling him that they would tear Jaime apart if he ever did anything to the women.

"That's messed up, man. Why haven't you said anything about this before, bro?" Joe asked. "You know I would do anything for you right?"

"I know you would, but this isn't any of your concern. I have hired additional protection and I even bought a gun for Celina. I just don't know what I would do if anything happened to them."

Meanwhile, the women were busy dancing the night away. Celina felt the same way as Fernando. She was having a hard time having fun. Paulina was the first to notice when she approached her.

"What's the matter sweetie? Are you nervous about tomorrow?"

"No I'm fine," she said faking a smile. "I just feel a little weird not being with Fernando tonight. Has he texted you?"

Paulina fumbled through her purse to find her phone and said "Nope. He hasn't." Then it dawned on her why her thoughts might be elsewhere.

"It's Jaime, isn't it?"

Celina shook her head slowly, telling her again how sorry she was for allowing him to do the things he had done over the last month.

"It's not your fault," Paulina said trying to comfort her.

"He would have found you no matter what."

"Hey, what's going on over here?" Angelica asked. This is supposed to be fun. Why aren't ya'll dancing?"

"I think we should go," Paulina apologized. "We just have a lot on our minds and have so much to do tomorrow. Let's just finish this round and head back to the house, all right?"

"Are you sure?"

"Yes, I'm sure. Besides, we don't want to have bags under our eyes for tomorrow," Paulina joked.

Both Celina and Paulina shared a bad feeling as if something was about to happen to them. As they sat there and polished off their drinks, they kept glancing at the dance floor and looking behind their shoulders, sensing something was wrong. They hallucinated that men walking by looked like Jaime.

Even as they left the bar, some of the cars that passed by seemed to look like the one Jaime drove. The night had a clouded feel to it as they made their way back to the ranch, and that fogged their attitude. Paulina and

Celina went straight to their rooms, still apologizing to everyone for ruining their night.

The women told them there was no need to apologize and to just relax and how they should get some beauty rest for the next day. The men also called it an early night going back to the hotel before midnight.

The day finally arrived. It was a beautiful morning in Texas and the weather couldn't have been better. After going in to town for breakfast, the men went to the tuxedo shop to pick up their clothes and to meet the photographer downtown. They took a few pictures in their suits and tails, having a good time laughing and joking about who was going to wed next.

Andy asked to speak to Fernando alone for a second to say something that was on his mind. He said "I know you don't take me too seriously at times, but there's something I have been wanting to tell you."

Fernando set all his silliness aside for a moment and allowed his friend to say what was on his mind.

"What's up?"

"I just wanted to say how much I admire you. Really. No matter what people may say about what you're doing here, it really is very noble of you to take Celina on the way you have. Not too many men would do such a thing. I know I couldn't."

"Like what do you mean? I'm not sure I understand." Fernando asked.

"Well, if more people like you could get past the jealousies and indifferences, I think marriages would make it a lot further," Andy knew his friend was not quite following him.

"Okay look, you and Paulina are a terrific couple, yeah? And here you have Celina who kept meeting all of those loser boyfriends, right? At the rate she was going, she in all likelihood would have never met the right guy who would love her and treat her like I know your lot will. How great it is of Paulina to share her husband and the life that you all have made for each other, with Celina. Am I making sense?"

Fernando smiled. "I think I know what you're trying to say, and I appreciate it. I think we all know a woman like Celina. Someone who kept attracting the same type of man who didn't appreciate her or treat her like she deserved to be treated. And I couldn't agree with you more that Paulina is maybe one in a million women who could see that Celina deserved better and could in fact share the life we made for each other with her. Women are very beautiful and mysterious creatures and I love and respect them all."

Then in an effort to try and make light of their conversation, Fernando said, "But I think most men these days tend to forget about that beautiful piece of flesh that surrounds a vagina."

Andy looked at him, waiting for his friend to finish. He waited a few seconds before asking, "What's that, Fernando?"

"A woman." Fernando said, at his most charming.

"Men these days only care about one thing and one thing only, and their missing out on one of the greatest treasures on earth—a woman."

Andy laughed at Fernando, because he knew that what he said was true.

As they started to make their way back to the other guys, Andy looked at his friend and said, "And, oh yeah, one more thing, I know this is Texas and all, and I've heard of a Texas two-step before, but I have never heard of a Texas three-step."

Back at the ranch, Paulina and Celina inadvertently woke up extra early to put the final touches to their wedding vows. The other women were getting ready so the brides could take them to a beauty salon for a morning of pampering and to have their nails done before heading in to town.

They had about three hours before they would be wed, but neither showed a case of the butterflies. Things were going just as they were meant to be.

In no time, the women had their nails done and began their descent into downtown to the hotel.

Guests were starting to arrive including co-workers, family and friends. When they got there, Rhonda took Paulina and Celina straight to a dressing area she had reserved so they could get ready. Paulina confidently began to dress while Celina headed straight to the bathroom to release the nervous butterflies from her stomach. She shut the door behind her and began to hug the toilet, trying not to ruin her makeup. With all that was happening, Celina had become nauseated over the last few days and was glad it was all about to be over soon.

She fumbled through her purse to find something she stored away that she bought at a local pharmacy as Paulina gently tapped on the door. "Are you all right? Is everything okay?"

"Yes I'm fine. I'll just be a minute."

Everyone else began to mingle in the reception room talking about how beautifully decorated it was. The room was aromatic with white and pink and roses that softly blanketed the illustrious banquet hall. The tables were draped with white linen and featured white china with silver rims, crystal glasses that matched the crystal chandeliers overhead and sterling silver flatware. Every table had a three-tier candelabra, flaming long white candles and a bottle of champagne chilling in pewter coolers.

Soon, guests filled the room, with the exception of Paulina's parents who kept their word and did not attend. The security guards were not there either as Fernando felt this was a private event, and they would have no need for their protection.

Caterers were going in and out of the room bringing in last minute dishes while uniformed servers passed around hors d'oeuvres and filled champagne glasses. Next, Rhonda walked into the room and asked everyone to please take their seats and instructed the wedding party to take their position near the front of the room by an archway.

At her cue, Johann Sebastian Bach's Canon in D by Johann Pachelbel began to play.

Paulina entered the room first. She wore a variation of her original wedding dress. The beautiful, strapless gown had a fitted ruche bodice with a sweetheart neckline, accented by original hand-beaded and embroidered pearls and lace. Pale, pink silk and American tulle flowers gathered the skirt at the back, drawing attention to the long elegant train. Paulina wore her hair in long waves down her back with small white flowers braided into sections of the waves. She carried a small bouquet of white roses and pink Asiatic lilies.

Next, Celina walked in, wearing a simple, long-sleeved, silvery satin gown that had very little detail in front, but the back of the gown took everyone's breath away. There was an ornate cut out between the middle of Celina's shoulder blades all the way down to the waistline of the gown. The cutout was framed with lace flowers and pearl beads. There were buttons that began at the nape of her neck all the way down to the end of the hem of the short train. The sleeves had buttons that ran down the length of her forearms. In her arms, she also carried a bouquet of white roses and Asiatic lilies; however, Paulina felt that since this was Celina's special day, she should carry a much larger one than herself. Celina's hair was swept off her shoulders in a soft "up do" accented with a silver tiara adorned with pearls, crystals and white roses.

They stood on either side of Fernando, each glancing in each other's eyes. He reached out and took each of them by the hand and squeezed them softly in his.

Enchanted, he whispered how beautiful they looked as their eyes began to dampen with tears. Everyone's focus was fixed on the three of them as they stood there for the entire world to see. Their love and admiration for one another was going to be forever bound as they were about to make known to those present to witness their vows.

Paulina began. "I wanted to begin by saying how much I love and care for you two with all my heart. In the short while we all have been together, we have faced and overcome some very trying times. Yet it has been our love for one another that has sustained us. Because of that, I know that we have what it takes to make it through whatever this life may bring us. I have known Fernando for twelve years now and being with him has been the best thing that has ever happened to me. Our love has continued to grow more and more over the years and now God has found a new way to express His love and guidance by bringing Celina into our family."

She looked at Celina and said, "I vow to love and cherish you as I have loved and cherished my husband. I welcome you into my family and into my heart."

With a trembling voice Celina said in return, "Since meeting the two of you, I have experienced so many changes. But the greatest change of all has been discovering what love really is. When you two came into my life, I was on an uncertain path. For the first time in my life, I feel like I belong somewhere and to someone…or some two," Celina smiled as the crowd giggled. My life will never be the same because I am whole now. With you, I'm complete. I vow to love and cherish you both, all of my life."

Fernando looked into both their eyes and hesitated for a moment before feeling the warmth of their love pass through his chest. He inhaled and said with a strong voice, "I am so blessed to have such wonderful women in my life. No words can express the love and appreciation I have for the two of you. All I have ever done has led me here to this moment, and there is nothing I wouldn't do for either of you. I will let nothing, for as long as I live, come between my love for each of you. As we stand here today in the presence of God, our family, and our friends, I vow my commitment to each of you from this day forward, to love, honor and protect you both for the rest of my days as your husband…"

A commotion from the back of the room began to develop as the banquet doors suddenly swung open.

An obviously troubled man rushed by the crowd and yelled from the top of his voice, "CELINA!!!!!!"

Fernando pulled the women closer to him, sheltering them behind him. The crowd began to stand in total confusion, trying to make sense of what was going on. As the man ran closer to the front, he reached into his coat pocket and pulled out a gun, cocked the trigger back, and aimed it at Fernando.

Then suddenly, the gun went off.

People in the crowd began to yell and scream in frenzy. The gunman, in full wrath, then pointed the gun at Celina who was kneeling down at Fernando's side. Just as the gunman was about to pull the trigger, Joe and Andy tackled him. The men wrestled him to the floor, as Paulina and Celina knelt next to Fernando, and Katy and Paul rushed out to get help.

Celina cried out, "Please somebody help us!"

Without hesitation, Angelica rushed over to Fernando to inspect his injuries. He appeared to have been shot in the chest. His breathing became shallow and labored. He reached out to Paulina and tried to speak. Paulina grabbed his hand and said, "Don't talk, babe. Angie is going to take care of you."

She looked over to Celina who had both hands pressed against Fernando's chest and saw the frightened look upon her face as the blood continued to flow. Then Paulina firmly placed her hands over Celina's as Fernando's face became ashen and pale.

"I'm dying he whispered," as tears welled up in his eyes.

"No!" Paulina cried. "No you can't die. And do you know why?"

She said as she fought back her tears. "Because you going to be a father."

He firmly held on to her hand as tears began to run down the side of his face.

"That's right, babe. I'm pregnant," she said smiling at him.

Celina's eyes lit up as she looked at them and remembered something in her purse she wanted to show them that she had just found out only moments before. "Fernando, you're going to make it, honey. Hang in there, baby. I have something to show you."

She looked up into the crowd and asked "Will someone please grab my purse? It's in the dressing room."

Jessica heard her cries and, in a moment's time, she handed her purse to her. Celina quickly dumped out all the contents and picked up a home pregnancy test she bought at the pharmacy just days before. "Look baby, it's blue. I'm pregnant, too."

After learning he was about to be a father, Fernando tried his best to hang in there. Looking up at his brides, he tried to tell them how much he loved them, but his wound was too severe.

The more he tried, the weaker be became. With only a faint pulse, he lost conscienceless just before the paramedics got there. They tried everything they could to keep him alive, but he had lost a lot of blood and they didn't know if he would make it or not. Fortunately, the hospital was only minutes away.

Joe and Andy kept a watchful eye on the gunman as they kept him at bay long enough for the police to take him into custody. Later he would be identified as twenty-four year old Jaime Luis Mata of New York City. After hours of questioning, he finally told the police of his intent to murder Celina and his rage against Fernando for taking his girlfriend away from him. He would be tried and convicted of two counts of attempted murder and sentenced to twenty years in prison.

Over the next year, Paulina and Celina continued to work together at the gallery, expanding the business to nearby Dallas in the historic Deep Ellum district.

Their children, Esteban Miguel and Emily Ann De la Mar spent their first year at home with their father who recovered from his wounds after many months of physical therapy and plenty of rest. He would need his strength for what he planned to do next, which was to enter into politics and make a stand to the government to protect their rights and belief in the institution of plural marriage.

Made in the USA
Charleston, SC
19 July 2012